I0718379

Float:
Enchanted Horse
Retold

DEMELZA CARLTON

A tale in the Romance a Medieval Fairy Tale series

DEDICATION

This one is for my daughter.
If not for her, I never would have fallen face-first into
a gondola.
Or fallen in love with Venice and its incredible history.

One

"Don't mess this up," Godfrey muttered, as if being stern with himself could stop the inevitable. Easier to stop the waves carrying his boat to Lord Sebastiano's door, or to command the gondolier to plant his pole so as to resist the tide. A stealthy glance at the gondolier confirmed Godfrey's fears – the man thought him mad, talking to himself.

The boat turned into one of Rialto's numerous identical canals, weaving through the maze as if by magic, until they stopped at a dock that looked no different to the others they'd passed.

"Palazzo Ziano," the gondolier said, offering his hand to Godfrey like his passenger was some fine lady.

Godfrey choked out a laugh and stepped from the boat to the dock without the boatman's assistance. A few coins changed hands and the gondolier poled away, disappearing around a corner before Godfrey could reconsider and call him back.

Godfrey eyed the double doors before him. Paint peeled at the bottom, where the wood had swelled in response to the endless stroking of the waves that even now threatened to lick tantalisingly at his feet. He rapped on the timber with more confidence than he felt, fuelled by desperation to keep his feet dry until he'd at least met with Lord Sebastiano.

The door opened inward, and a servant bowed him inside the cavernous space that evidently served as a warehouse for whatever Sebastiano traded in, when he wasn't transporting things for people.

"I think I've come to the wrong place," Godfrey said. "You see, I'm in Rialto to see Lord Sebastiano about a cargo his ships were to carry here from the Holy Land. He invited me to visit him at home, but…" This evidently wasn't it. Perhaps the boatman had decided a mere baron's youngest son was not worthy to enter the home of one of the city's patricians.

"Up the stairs. What name shall I tell the master?" the servant asked.

Godfrey's eyes adjusted to the gloom. The wide staircase before him led to a more lordly entrance on the level above. Perhaps he was in the right place after all.

"Godfrey. My father, the Baron of Maraschal, sent me."

"If you will follow me, Master Godfrey?"

Up the stairs and into the house proper, Godfrey's fears fluttered about inside his chest. He didn't want to open his mouth for fear they'd fly out.

"Master Godfrey, the Baron of Maraschal's son," the servant boomed, then stood aside to let Godfrey pass into the room.

Lord Sebastiano rose and moved around his

desk to clasp Godfrey's hands in his. "Master Godfrey, it is a pleasure to meet you. Your uncle, Eustace, speaks well of you. He says you work magic with horses."

Godfrey hadn't seen Uncle Eustace in more than ten years, so how he could know such a thing...perhaps his father had sent him a letter. Yes, of course. A letter saying Godfrey would be collecting this shipment of horses.

"A pity you do not have the same power over ships. The convoy you are here for is a week overdue. It is likely nothing, but many cities along the coast have fallen to the Seljuks in the last few years. It would be ill luck indeed if they have attacked my ships..." Sebastiano patted Godfrey's hand before releasing him. "But it is a fool indeed who would attack such a well-armed convoy. Your horses will arrive safely, you'll see, and you'll have them home in time for Easter. Which reminds me...it is Carnevale this week, the final week of feasting before we fast. You must dine with us tonight."

Godfrey looked up to meet Sebastiano's expectant eyes. The invitation was no mere courtesy – the patrician wanted an answer. "I'd be honoured, and delighted," he managed to say.

Sebastiano smiled. "Good. You have caught me at a good time. I'd planned on visiting the harbour this afternoon. Will you accompany me?"

Godfrey could hardly refuse, and soon found himself back in a boat, moving with surprising swiftness across the lagoon.

Upon hearing that this was Godfrey's first visit to Rialto, Sebastiano maintained a running commentary about everything he saw, from the islands on either side of them to the people in the boats they passed to the fish in the lagoon waters below.

When Sebastiano paused for breath, Godfrey asked, "How long have your family ruled Rialto?"

Sebastiano laughed. "Ah, you must come from the barbarian kingdoms to the north. No one family rules Rialto. We are a republic, and our rulers are elected from among the noblest families in the city, her patricians. But it is no secret that my family can be traced back to

Ziano, one of the first twelve tribunes who ruled when our Most Serene Republic was formed, more than four hundred years ago. We have given the city three Dukes to date, and no doubt more will be elected in the future."

A republic? Like the ancient cities, burned and conquered by the Northmen who Sebastiano called barbarians. Yet this city still stood. A city without walls, as it spread across the islands of the lagoon, from the mainland to the harbour. A city so open should surely be an easy target.

"How does this city defend itself, without walls?"

Sebastiano reached over the side of the boat and cupped seawater in his hands. "The sea protects us, for she is as much a part of our city as the people in it. And there is no fiercer protector than a wife and mother defending her own family." He let the water cascade down his hands, trickling back into the lagoon. "And just like a man knows the body of his wife, the men of the lagoon know every channel and shoal, navigating skilfully across all the curves of the seabed. He knows her moods, her passions, and how to skim smoothly through her waves to the deep channels she opens only to him."

Godfrey felt his face grow hot. Likening the cold water to a lover…he'd sooner love a corpse. Maybe madness was part of being a man of Rialto. And yet, he could almost hear a woman's whisper in the waves, inviting him into her depths.

Godfrey shook his head. A foolish notion.

"If you have need of female company while you are in Rialto, I'm sure my sons can help you find a suitable courtesan," Sebastiano said.

Oh, by all that was holy…

Sebastiano laughed. "When I was your age, my father had already found me a bride. Are you betrothed yet, Master Godfrey?"

Wordlessly, Godfrey shook his head. He managed to find his voice. "My older brothers are already married, with babes on the way, so there is no need for me to marry, or produce more heirs. My father has had me managing the horse stud, so when Uncle Eustace was due to send some new breeding stock, he sent me to fetch them."

"Then after dinner tonight, my sons will find you a courtesan," Sebastiano said. When Godfrey opened his mouth to protest, Sebastiano held up his hand to silence him. "You are in Rialto, a city famed for the beauty of its women. I cannot in conscience allow you to leave this jewel of a city without tasting its delights."

Not wanting to anger his host – that would certainly mess things up – Godfrey decided to ask about the numerous posts and flags sticking out of the water. He opened his mouth.

"I think you are in luck, Master Godfrey. My ships have come to greet you." Sebastiano pointed.

A forest of masts grew on the horizon, separating out into more than a dozen ships. Godfrey wouldn't know one vessel from another, but Sebastiano nodded with satisfaction as he surveyed the convoy coming into the harbour.

By the time Godfrey and Sebastiano reached the ship they wanted, the docks were swarming with men, unloading the ships and taking cargo to smaller boats which then set off for the city. Where it would be stored in the warehouses beneath the merchants' homes, Godfrey realised, for there were no storehouses here in the harbour.

"And here are your horses!" Sebastiano said proudly, as he led the way across the gangplank to the deck which had been turned into a makeshift stable.

Six horses occupied the deck, each as magnificent as any other animal in his father's stable. Mounts befitting a king or an emperor, who would breed countless more when they reached home.

"My men will take them ashore to stretch their legs, then they shall board a barge to take them to the mainland. They will be waiting for you at the Sailor's Rest, the inn nearest the docks. The innkeeper there will take good care of them while you enjoy the legendary hospitality of Rialto," Sebastiano said.

And no doubt charge him a hefty sum for every day, Godfrey thought but did not say. In the merchant city of Rialto, everything cost more. His father had given him plenty of coin for the journey, but Godfrey was sure his purse did not run to weeks of revelry. Or the company of one of the city's courtesans.

If he needed a whore so badly, there were plenty in every tavern on the way home, at a fraction of the price. He could keep it in his hose until then.

A roar came from the stable, followed by an explosion of straw. "What do you think you're doing with my horses, boy?" An old man, clad in stained rags, emerged from the stable. "Watch her footing on the gangplank! She's worth more than your life, and if the mare should be injured…" For an old beggar, he had the commanding voice of a much younger man.

The unfortunate sailor leading the priceless mare ducked his head, as though avoiding a blow from the man.

"Tielo?"

Godfrey started at the sound of his father's nickname – something he'd only heard his mother use – and found the old man staring at him. "No, I'm Godfrey," he said.

The old man straightened, then grimaced. "Tielo's youngest boy?" He hobbled across the deck and down the gangplank until he stood before Godfrey, then peered up at him.

This man looked old enough to be his grandfather, instead of his father's younger brother, but Godfrey asked anyway: "Uncle Eustace? What are you doing here? Shouldn't you be in the Holy City?"

"The city has fallen to the Seljuks. I was returning from the harbour, where I'd just seen the horses loaded aboard, and they had the city surrounded. Besieged. They'd demolished one wall and you could hear the screams from a mile away. When I saw there was no hope, I turned around and headed back to the harbour, as fast as my horse would carry me. I had to get word out. The Pope must hear of this, and call for a new crusade to free the Holy City from the infidels!" He thrust his fist up into the air to emphasise his point, but this seemed to be more than his body could bear. Eustace fell to his knees and toppled over, out cold.

Sebastiano helped Godfrey haul the

unconscious man into a boat, suggesting he take his uncle to his lodgings and summon a healer to see to him. "He is also welcome to join us for dinner, if he recovers," Sebastiano said.

Godfrey mumbled something he hoped sounded obliging as he directed the boatman to the inn where he was staying. The breeze had picked up, whipping the lagoon into small, savage waves that soon woke Eustace. Godfrey could get no sense out of him, aside from a lengthy account of the state of the Holy City.

Men, women and children, chained up and sold into slavery, or slaughtered if they put up the slightest resistance. Oh, but not the women. Any woman who resisted was taken to entertain the soldiers, until they tired of her and left her lying in a pool of her own blood on the ground.

"Is this true?" the gondolier demanded.

Godfrey shook his head, but Eustace reared up. "Of course it's true! I saw it with my own eyes. Raping virgins in the Holy City. Savages, the lot of them. The Pope must hear of it, and call for all good men to put a stop to it! For the Holy Land to be so befouled..."

The gondolier's eyes widened, and he poled faster.

The sun was sinking by the time the healer left Godfrey's lodgings, having dressed the wounds hidden beneath Eustace's rags. He'd given Eustace a draught to make him sleep before extracting an arrowhead from one of the wounds and binding that, too.

"Will he be all right?" Godfrey asked.

The healer shrugged. "If I have stopped the infection in time, then yes. If one of the wounds festers...I shall return on the morrow."

Godfrey paid the man, then turned to watch his uncle snoring. Amid Eustace's babblings, he'd also told the tale of his escape from the city amid a storm of arrows, some of which had found their mark in his flesh. No wonder he looked twenty years older than Father, instead of ten years younger.

Sebastiano would understand if Godfrey did not turn up for dinner, he was sure. The patrician would accept his apologies. But that meant staying here, watching his uncle sleep, and worrying that he might not wake. Better that Godfrey go out for a while, and return when his uncle woke.

Godfrey dressed in clean garb, then summoned a boatman to take him to Palazzo Ziano for the second time that day.

He barely noticed the journey this time. He could not have answered whether the sun still shone or whether the waves wet him on the way, for all too soon he found himself at Sebastiano's doors. This time, he didn't hesitate to knock.

Sebastiano's dining chamber could have been the twin of the office he'd visited earlier in the day, with the low ceiling and cosy fire making it look like a private room in an inn instead of a nobleman's dining hall. Even the table where Sebastiano sat had benches on both sides, despite sitting on a dais.

"Please, sit," Sebastiano said, rising. He gestured toward the seat across from him. Only then did Godfrey realise what was wrong with the room – Sebastiano sat at what would be the place of honour on his father's table, but with benches on each side of the table, he was offering a seat of equal honour to his guest, and leaving the seat at the head of the table vacant. "How is your uncle?"

Godfrey blinked, bringing his thoughts back to his host and not the man's furniture. "He is resting. He was wounded. It looked like some of the enemy archers used him for target practice. The healer did what he could for him, but..." Godfrey didn't dare finish, for what could he say? That his uncle might die? Sebastiano was Eustace's friend. He would not like to hear such things any more than Godfrey wanted to say them.

Sebastiano nodded gravely. "Sometimes rest and time are better healers than all the potions in the world. Followed closely by the company of one's family, for which I must apologise. I know I promised you would meet my sons, but they – "

Sons. Courtesans. Godfrey had completely forgotten, yet it seemed Sebastiano had not. Did Sebastiano seriously think Godfrey would want to take some painted whore to the bed where his uncle lay dying?

Copper caught the candlelight, dazzling Godfrey into blindness. When he managed to blink away the lights in his eyes, what he saw stole his breath instead.

Soft copper waves floated above a sea the same shade of aqua blue as the lagoon outside, when the sun caressed the water. Her silk gown shimmered in the candlelight, cut as modestly as that belonging to some highborn matron, but the wicked fire in her eyes would have tempted the devil himself – she was no man's faithful wife.

If this woman was the courtesan Sebastiano's sons had chosen, they had plucked an angel from heaven, and he would fall to his knees and beg for a smile from such a paragon. Nay, he'd offer her every coin he possessed and pledge his life in servitude…

Her lips quirked, parting just the slightest bit, and Godfrey was consumed with the desire to kiss her. Kiss her until he ran out of breath, and then he might die happily.

He would sell his father's horses, and the clothes on his back, and then maybe, just maybe…

"May I present my daughter, Lady Penelope?" Sebastiano said.

Godfrey's mouth had dropped open at some point, and as his mind processed the patrician's words, horror locked his jaw so that he could not seem to close it. By all that was holy…he'd mistaken the patrician's daughter for a whore?

If Sebastiano or Lady Penelope knew his thoughts, they'd toss him out the door and straight into the canal to drown. It was the least he'd deserve for such an unforgivable insult.

"Some wine for our guest," Lady Penelope called, with a glance at Sebastiano. "Father, have you not offered him any refreshment yet? What will he think of such poor hospitality?" She accepted a jug of wine from a servant, and poured a goblet for herself, before offering her own cup to Godfrey. A wicked smile lifted her lips. "Please, drink. My father is lucky you did not threaten to toss him into the canal for such an insult."

Godfrey lifted the wine to his lips, then choked on the first mouthful as her words registered. Either she'd read his mind, or his thoughts were written so plainly across his face, she hadn't needed to. Any moment now, her father would draw his sword and…

"Ah, Vitale, my friend, so good you could join us. Master Godfrey, this is Duke Vitale, the ruler of Rialto. I had hoped he might hear from your uncle the state of affairs in the Holy Land, but as he is not feeling well…"

Godfrey jumped to his feet, bowing at the newcomer. He would not have picked the Duke as any higher rank than Sebastiano, for the only difference between the men's garb was an embroidered cloth hat the Duke wore.

"Have you come from the Holy Land?" the Duke demanded.

Godfrey shook his head. "No, I have come from the north, but my uncle has told me much of what happened to the city. Perhaps you will allow me to tell you what I can remember."

The Duke sat. "Please do."

Keeping his eyes firmly fixed on the Duke, Godfrey began to repeat his uncle's tales.

For if he looked at her again, he would lose

his very soul to her spell.

Two

Penelope stared at the boy Father had invited to dinner. The boy who thought she was the most beautiful woman he'd ever seen, an angel, and a courtesan. As though anyone could be all three.

She'd considered accidentally knocking his cup over, covering his clothes in wine, but there was no wine on the table yet. Mother would not have forgotten such a thing, but she had left this world two summers ago, and supped at a more heavenly feast than this one would be.

The boy's thoughts turned to how much he'd like to kiss her. Kiss her, and that was all. She'd never met a boy with thoughts so chaste, though she'd read the minds of most of the men in the city, whether she liked it or not. Truth be told, she did not like it, for she'd probably seen more debauchery in their thoughts than any brothel in the city. Her father would be horrified if he knew his virgin daughter could describe over a dozen ways to pleasure a man with her hands and mouth alone…and what prices the whores in town charged for such things.

Luckily, her father had no idea she could read minds, and she intended to keep it that way. So she sat silently, listening to the boy's tales of war and the world outside of Rialto, and wished that one day, she might travel beyond the lagoon. Though not to the Holy Land, by the sound of things, where women were raped, chained, separated from their children, raped again, then sold into slavery where they were likely to never know a night alone in their own bed again. Unlike the whores of Rialto, who could suck enough money out of newly arrived sailors to take the occasional night off…often to meet lovers of their own choosing. Noblemen who might marry them, or at least keep them as courtesans or mistresses, free of the street and sailors.

Everyone dreamed of something, and she was no stranger to those thoughts, either.

This boy – Godfrey, his name was – feared his dreams would be nightmares about the fall of the Holy City. Things of blood and darkness. When he departed that night, he barely glanced at her, so dark were his thoughts that he'd entirely forgotten her existence.

Father invited him to dine with them again, every night he was in the city, and Penelope made sure to sit where she might hear him speak, though he never said a word to her. His uncle was ill, she learned, and as soon as he was well enough to travel, they would both leave. Until then, her father intended to keep the boy in his household as much as possible. She thought little of it, until she caught her brothers discussing Godfrey with their father one day.

"She is too young!"

"We cannot afford it!"

"If we hadn't sent that expedition to the northern seas, perhaps we could afford it, or if it had returned, but it's been a year and there is no word…"

Seeing herself in her brothers' thoughts, Penelope concentrated harder.

Her father had always been one for hiding his thoughts, but his words were clear enough. "Your mother had already given me a son when she was her age. In this house, with your wives and children, do you not think she wants to have the same for herself?"

"But she brings nothing to the household! We take care of your business, Father, bringing wealth in. What will she do but take it away to some other rival family?" That was Pietro, the youngest of her brothers. He'd married a thirty-year-old widow he could not stand the sight of for the size of her dowry alone. She suspected he'd rather stick his manhood into a bag of gold and get his pleasure that way than go anywhere near his wife.

Domenico was the oldest and most reasonable, so it was no surprise to hear him say, "Perhaps a widower without an heir…someone who has more need of a young, fertile wife, than any kind of dowry."

"No. I will not send Penelope into a miserable marriage, where she will be widowed young."

"Perhaps you should ask Penelope who she wants to marry," Orso suggested, trying hard not to laugh. "If she has a particular old man in mind, maybe she won't be miserable. She spends all her time weaving and sewing. Maybe a wool merchant, or one who sells silk…Ha, or a lace merchant, where she can learn to make Rialto's finest lace for pure profit, just like in the stories." He liked to stir up trouble, tossing out the idea more to see Father's reaction than anything else, but there was a tiny grain of hope that Father might accept his idea. Sending a convoy north had been his idea, and the loss gnawed at him.

"Enough!" Father said. "I will choose who Penelope marries, not any of you. Whether she marries another patrician, or some patrician's son, or even some foreign nobleman, the decision is mine to make."

Penelope had long ago come to terms with this, though she'd raged against it as a child. Now, she was more interested in her father's thoughts, in which she could see a clear picture of Godfrey. He was the foreign nobleman he had in mind.

That night at dinner, she watched Godfrey, and was surprised to see how many times he gazed at her before looking away again. But he was less successful at turning his thoughts away from her. In fact, he thought about her with such ardour it was enough to warm her cheeks, though his thoughts never strayed to anything more passionate than a kiss. And the more he thought about kissing her, the more she warmed to the idea.

She retired early that night, but she could not sleep. Was Father seriously considering marrying her to that boy? She had to admit, she liked him better than most of the other men she'd met, but not to the point of passion, or love. Her brothers and even her father might scoff at such a notion, but she'd read the thoughts of enough people to know there were love matches, and marriages where passion played a big part. They were rare, true, but not unknown. She'd tasted Godfrey's eager desire for her, so why could she not arouse the same passion in herself at the thought of him?

When the next day dawned, she resolved to find her father, and ask him whether he meant to marry her to Godfrey.

But she slept late, and by the time she made her way to the dining chamber, her father and brothers had gone, leaving her to break her fast alone. Servants brought her bread, oil and fruit. She ripped off a piece of bread, dipped it on the oil and munched on it slowly, eyeing the bowl of fruit with distaste. It looked like last year's peaches swimming in honey, much too sweet for her taste. No, she longed for the first spring peaches, fresh picked from the tree, and summer berries, so bursting with juice they stained her fingers, but this winter didn't seem to want to end.

"Do we have any oranges?" she asked.

Silence greeted her – the servants had all gone, to do whatever duties they normally did this late in the morning. She sighed. Her brothers' wives would have just repeated the question, louder, until a servant produced what the woman wanted, but Penelope had grown up in this house with these servants, and most of them still saw her as a child. A child who had been in trouble many more times for climbing the trees in the orchard than for raising her voice.

She stopped to wrap a cloak around her shoulders from the hook by the door before heading outside into the garden. Frost rimed the trees, making her wish she'd grabbed gloves as well, but that would only take longer. She wanted oranges now, not later.

Penelope surveyed the trees, but there was no low hanging fruit today. No, all the ripe oranges were higher up, where the sun kissed them. Ah, she could do with a little sun, too. And it wasn't like anyone was watching...

She found a ladder frozen to one of the tree trunks, but didn't have the strength to pry it free, so she climbed it instead, stepping into the canopy as easily as she would if it was the landing at the top of the stairs. It had been years since she'd climbed trees, but she hadn't forgotten. She tested each branch before putting her weight on it, reaching higher and higher until she found a clump of oranges as red as the sun. She twisted them free and stuffed the cold globes into the pockets of her cloak until she could not carry any more. Then she made her way down to the ground again.

"Is no one home? He demands to see the master!"

"Lord Sebastiano and his sons are at the Ducal Palace, and the wives are all visiting their families today."

"What about Lady Penelope?"

"I brought her breakfast in the dining room myself, but now she's nowhere to be found."

"If it's someone important, perhaps you should send a boy down to the Palace to fetch the master. Who is it?"

"That boy who has dined here all week, making moon eyes at Lady Penelope. Godefroi, or some barbarous northern name like it."

Godfrey. If Penelope couldn't ask her father, perhaps she could ask the boy himself if they had a betrothal cooked up between them.

She crept down the ladder, jumping down the last few rungs to land with an audible thump on the frozen ground. She strode toward the two servants, lifting her head high as she hoped they would not question her. "Send him into the dining chamber. I will greet him, hear whatever message he has for my father, and see him on his way," Penelope ordered, not breaking stride as she swept into the house.

She barely had time to drop her orange-burdened cloak beneath the table before she had to turn and greet Godfrey.

He looked like he'd had less sleep than her, but there was nothing in his thoughts to tell her why.

"My lady," he breathed, bowing low. The only image in his head was of her – her hair haloing her like some sort of angel, with a crown of…

She swore under her breath and desperately tried to comb the leaves out of her hair before he looked at her again.

"Would you like some refreshment? Bread,

fruit…wine?" she asked.

He stared fixedly at the floor, shaking his head. "I cannot. My uncle died of his wounds last night, and I must return home. His final wish was to be buried in our family crypt, and I gave my word."

Her hands flew to her mouth. "Heavens, Master Godfrey, I'm so sorry. May God rest his soul. I'm sure he was a good man, as are you for granting his wish."

He looked up in surprise. "Thank you, my lady. You are kind to say so. I wish I could have stayed longer." For her, his thoughts added. "But I must bid you farewell, and I'd hoped to give your father my apologies, too, for leaving with so little warning."

She took her hands in his. "I will tell him all you have told me. On my father's behalf, as well as my own, I wish you a safe journey home."

"Thank you. I pray I will be able to return soon, for your father and the Duke both assured me that the men of Rialto will take up the crusade to free the Holy Land, and I have no doubt that once the rest of Christendom hears, thousands more will take up their swords to defend the faith. When the trade routes open again, I shall return." He lifted her hands to his lips and kissed them.

Her skin tingled as though his lips burned her…and yet, she did not want to pull away.

Nor did he. He wanted to take her with him – had intended to ask her father for her hand. But now he was in mourning for his uncle, he could not.

Could she marry this man she barely knew? If he'd asked for her today, could she have borne sharing a bed with him?

There was one way to find out. She wet her lips, marching forward to close the distance between them. Godfrey dropped her hands and backed away, but she followed, backing him up against the wall. Now or never.

She seized his shoulders and kissed him. Though she'd experienced a thousand kisses in the thoughts of others, this was the first one that had touched her lips. Clumsy at first, for he was as inexperienced as she, but not for long. Passion took over, and she wasn't sure if it was his or hers, rushing through her like flames, as her body pressed against his and they kissed again.

He was all lean and hard, in all the right places, but his touch was gentle as he pulled her close, and deepened the kiss.

Images of ships and armies crowded her mind, thoughts that had nothing to do with her or Godfrey, as someone else approached the dining chamber.

Her father and brothers!

Reluctantly, she pulled away, straightening her clothes as she put a decorous distance between them. Godfrey might want to marry her, and he kissed like the very devil himself, but her father had not agreed to a betrothal yet.

But she would. He had only to ask.

Godfrey heard the approaching voices and his confused expression vanished, to be replaced by calm composure.

When her father entered the room, Godfrey bowed and took his leave. He shot one meaningful glance at Penelope, who heard his vow to return for her as surely as if he'd spoken the words aloud, before he departed.

Penelope forced out a smile. "So what did the Duke have to say? Are we to save the Holy Land?"

Father sighed heavily. "He will raise an army, and a fleet to carry them. They will depart in the spring."

She ignored the doubts shadowing his thoughts. "Then Duke Vitale will free them all by the summer, and Master Godfrey will return." She tried to believe the words with all her might, but they rang hollow.

"With no family left here or in the Holy Land, Godfrey has no need to return. Even if the Holy City is ours again by summer, I doubt we will ever see him again."

She stopped dead. "But…I thought you planned for me to marry him. I heard you say…"

Domenico choked on his ale and Orso laughed aloud. Pietro's brow just scrunched together like he wanted to shout at her, but didn't dare.

Father shook his head. "Our fortunes would have to be in a sorry state indeed before I allowed you to marry some foreign horse trader. No, you will marry a man worth of you, my little duck. But not for some time."

Penelope longed for her father to be wrong, but she knew in her heart that he was not.

It would be three years before she saw Godfrey again. Three years that saw Duke Vitale and his grand army to their graves, and a new crusade had begun.

And the world would never be the same.

Three

"Crusaders must be the most saintly knights in Christendom," Melisende said dreamily. "I'm surprised you aren't going to join them, now you're a knight, Godfrey. Isn't knighthood all about honour? Travelling so far from home to lay down your very life to save the Holy City…so honourable you cannot help but be named a saint."

"More like the least saintly," Father interrupted, setting down his wine cup. "Though I have no doubt Godfrey earned his knighthood with honour, the truth of knighthood is little more than being able to sit upon a horse without falling off, and knowing one end of a sword from the other. Most of them have only taken up the cross for the glory of it, or the promised pardon of all their sins. They are men who are not heroes at home, or who have no hope of heaven without a good deed so great, it erases everything else they have done. Younger sons and troublemakers – those their fathers would not miss, if they do not return. Unlike my sons, who are very much needed here at home." He signalled for a servant to refill his wine cup. "I am delighted that none of your brothers have decided to join this fool scheme."

Too busy dealing with the damage and thievery those supposed saints had wreaked as they rode across Father's lands, Godfrey mused silently. His brothers still had not returned, so he was the only one of Father's sons in the dining hall that day. Probably because he was the youngest, his knighthood so newly minted that he didn't yet answer when someone addressed him as Sir Knight. He could handle a horse and a sword, but little else, so it was no wonder he was not yet trusted enough to act on his own, like his older brothers.

Especially after his first solo task for his father had resulted in the death of Uncle Eustace and the end of all trade with the Holy Land. No one wanted that sort of ill luck again, so Godfrey was kept on a short rein, close to home.

He did not mind. His brothers would manage the estate, while he could focus on what he did best – working with the horses. His great grandfather had brought home some particularly fine horses when he went crusading, before Uncle Eustace had lost his life bringing more, and they'd bred a herd that was the envy of kings and emperors alike. Kings and emperors who were only too happy to buy the beasts when they came up for sale. The new colt that was born last week came from two particularly good bloodlines. If he could train it as well as he had the beast's sisters, he would be a mount fit for a king. Perhaps tomorrow…

"Godfrey!"

Godfrey blinked, focussing on his father. "Yes?"

"Tell your sister what the crusading army has done."

Fathered a bunch of bastards on as many girls as they could find, Godfrey thought but daren't say. No, Melisende should not hear about the plague of brutal rapes that had beset their lands. He wondered what would happen when their pack of rapists met the army of Seljuk ones. All one side had to do was don dresses and hide their weapons beneath them and victory would be assured, for the other army would be caught with their hose about their ankles. That would be a sight to see.

Ah…what had Father asked again? Oh, that's right.

"They slaughtered and ate a herd of dairy cows in the next village – nothing left – and then burned one of the wheat fields with one of their roasting fires, days before harvest. Other villages have lost all their poultry. One tavern brought out all their barrels of beer – which the crusaders took off with, not paying the tavernkeeper a single copper." And when he'd protested, the knights had laughed, seized the man's wife and daughters and…Godfrey swallowed. "We've kept the horses in the walled yard, instead of letting them out into the fields, so they don't see them. This army is like ants, taking and devouring everything in their path. It will be good when they are gone."

"They're camped outside town for now, but they'll ride on tomorrow," Father said. "Then they will be someone else's problem."

Godfrey glanced at Melisende, whose attention was fixed on her food. She probably hadn't heard a word. Her mind flew from one idea to another like a butterfly in a field full of flowers. He wished he could think as quickly as she could, but he suspected that if anyone else's mind worked as lightning-fast as hers, it would surely explode.

When he was done eating, he excused himself to go check on the horses.

He found them restless, annoyed at having to take their turns running about the walled yard, stuck in the stables for longer than they were accustomed. Good thing he'd brought a sack of early apples to share. He took his time, giving treats and stroking flanks, whispering promises of time in the fields tomorrow, until he was satisfied that he'd calmed them enough for the night.

And night it was, for darkness had fallen by the time he left the stables. Even the grooms had gone to bed. If he had any sense, he should do the same.

He bypassed the Great Hall, taking the servants' stairs up to the family chambers. He made it halfway up before he encountered a ghost.

The ghost squeaked, then lowered her white wool hood and whispered, "Godfrey! What are you doing here? Looming out of the darkness like that, you nearly made me scream and wake the whole house!"

"I'm going to bed. Where are you going?" he asked.

Melisende tossed her head, pressing her lips together with all the obstinacy Godfrey knew well.

"If you don't tell me, I'll be forced to tell Father, and he'll send men out to bring you back," Godfrey warned.

Her eyes widened in horror. "Oh, don't tell Father!" She grasped his arm with both hands. "Swear you will not tell Father, and I will tell you."

"Are you meeting a lover?" he demanded, feeling foolish the moment the words left his mouth.

Her expression turned thunderous. "Swear to me, Godfrey, or I shall tell you nothing."

She might be his younger sister, and much smaller than himself, but she made up for it in the breadth of her stubbornness. This was a battle Godfrey could not win.

He sighed, exhaling from the very depths of his soul. "Very well. I swear I shall not tell Father."

She nodded. "I am going up to St Michael's Spire, to watch the army march out on the morrow."

It was Godfrey's turn to nod. The Spire was a tower on the highest point around. A monastery had once stood there, since fallen into ruin, but the belltower remained, manned by guards from Father's own men. Melisende would sleep as safely there as here at home.

Perhaps even more so, for there was little to tempt the crusaders up the winding path to the mountain eyrie.

"Would you like me to come with you to protect you on the road?" Godfrey asked.

She snorted. "Of course not. With your big boots clomping along beside me, everyone from the castle to the town will know there's someone on the road alone, ripe for robbing. If I go alone, no one will even know I was there."

He hung his head. She had always been the stealthiest of Father's children — a better hunter than any of her brothers. He suspected she had inherited their mother's gift for magic, though he'd never seen her cast a spell. "As you wish." He headed up the stairs, turning sideways to squeeze past her.

Her hand against his shoulder halted him. "Godfrey." Her eyes held hurt. "You're a good and honourable knight, but you cannot protect everyone. We both know my fate will take me far from here."

Yes, but Father had not said who she would marry yet. Though he would soon, for she was of an age for a husband. She'd be a castle chatelaine, managing an estate as large as this one for her husband. While Godfrey stayed home, breeding horses instead of heirs, and his brothers managed Father's estate.

"Safe journey," he managed to say, before resuming his ascent. He swore as he stumbled and nearly fell.

"You, too, brother," he heard Melisende say from far below.

Four

Sun shone on the lagoon today, turning the usually grey waters into aquamarine so clear Penelope fancied she could see the fish swimming in it. The slight warmth made her think spring might finally come to the lagoon after this cold winter. Her foolish thought was whirled away in a gust of wintry wind that had her pulling her wool cloak more closely about her. No, spring would be a long time coming, for Carnevale had just begun and it would run for weeks yet.

Already, the nuns greeted the day's visitors

with gasps and shrieks, for most of them were masked. She stood on the island shore, away from the dock, knowing she would not receive any visitors today. Her father was a busy man, now he was the newly crowned Duke of Rialto, working hard to give the people the peace he had promised.

He'd granted her peace, too – the day after his coronation, he'd sent her here to the convent at Saint Angelo of Concordia, where she had naught but nuns and weaving to keep her occupied until she married.

Or so he thought.

"The green cloak suits you. I'm glad you like it."

So lost had Penelope been in her own thoughts, she hadn't heard his approaching footsteps, nor noticed the man in his familiar mask. At least he wasn't wearing the hat. The hat no one could clean the previous duke's blood from completely. Poor Duke Vitale, to survive war and plague, only to die on an assassin's blade as he stepped out of his own front door to go to mass.

Penelope dropped a graceful curtsey.

"Monsignor was most kind to send me such a gift for Yule. The convent here is much colder than the Ducal Palace." She lifted her face to the breeze. "Perhaps it is the wind coming off the water."

The eyes behind the mask tightened in concern. "If you need warmer clothes, furs, more wine, only say, and it will be yours. But I cannot let you come home. It is not safe."

Father feared he would be the next to fall to an assassin's knife, and he wished to spare her the sight of his mangled body. On the slim chance that his fears were realised, she didn't want to see him bathed in blood, either, so she allowed him the lie.

"Whereas here, I am so safe, the worst I shall do is catch a chill. Unless I catch a husband soon," she said.

She did not need to read her father's mind to know it would not be soon. His heavy sigh told its own tale.

"Would you prefer to be a princess, or remain a lady here in Rialto?" Father asked.

No mention of Godfrey. Not any more.

She should forget him, and mostly, she had,

except when talk turned to marriage, or the need for Father to make her a princess.

There were no kings in Rialto – the Duke reigned with his Council of the Wise until he died, or resigned. She was the nearest thing to a princess in the whole Republic. To truly make her a princess, Father would have to marry her off to some foreign prince, sending her far from home to form an alliance that would help Rialto.

"I would prefer to be the wife of a good husband, like you were to Mother," Penelope said.

Off came the mask. The Duke was done hiding his face. "If Vitale were still alive, I might be able to give you that. But now…we are beset by enemies on all sides. If your marriage could bring us peace in but one quarter…I must try." He did not say how much he feared for his life, for he was not the sort of warrior Duke Vitale had been, to lead an army to victory. Only to lose that army to a plague, and his life to an assassin's blade. He'd been Father's friend, too.

"Any word on which quarter it will be,

Father?" she asked. She plucked the names from his head as they appeared. "Otto or Frederick of Aachen, Alexios of Byzas…" She wanted to add Godfrey's name to the list, but after Duke Vitale had failed to free any of the captured cities, let alone the Holy Land, there had been no word from Godfrey or his family for three years. He'd probably forgotten all about her, marrying some northern girl who popped out fat babies like a hen laying eggs.

"Not Frederick! His father is trying to marry him to some southern spinster princess, sole heir to the throne, so he can have the southern Northmen's crown."

Not Frederick, then. And not someone in the south, either, if they had no men for her to marry.

"Who, then?"

Another heart-weary sigh. "If I had an answer, I would give it to you. The negotiations are slow, taking many months for letters to pass between my court and theirs. And some of our envoys have been detained…" Father closed his mouth before he could say more.

Penelope lifted the words from his head instead: "…detained and imprisoned by the Emperor or his vassals. And those who are released are almost unrecognisable…" At the image Father began to conjure in his mind, she shut his thoughts out as best she could. What she could not ignore was his shudder of horror at the torture his men had been subjected to.

She had to marry someone. She hoped it would not be the same man responsible for torturing her countrymen. What such a man might do to her…

But princes had servants to do such things for them, surely. Men they employed to do the things no man could possibly take pleasure in.

She swallowed her unsavoury thoughts, focussing instead on her father. "Then I thank you for the visit, for I know how little time you have to spare now. I hope you will have an answer soon. In the meantime, I shall…weave a wedding dress fit for a princess." Penelope forced out a smile, finishing up with a curtsey.

Duke Sebastiano kissed her cheek before covering his face with his falcon mask once more. "You are a good girl. If only I had a dozen other daughters just like you. Maybe then I might make peace with everyone."

"If anyone can find a way, you can," she said, more out of love than a belief that she was telling the truth. Her father was a good man. If there was a path out of the political chaos the world had become, she knew he would work day and night to find it, or at least the man who could.

Despite her green cloak, she did not envy him a bit.

Five

Godfrey tried to sleep, but he couldn't stop worrying about Melisende. The crusader army was camped on the other side of town from both the Spire and the castle, but he'd seen plenty of evidence that not all the men stayed in the camp. He should have gone with her, or broken his oath and told his father anyway.

If anything happened to her, he would never forgive himself.

Finally, he rose, not caring who heard him on his way to the stable in the predawn darkness. He woke Pegasus, the swiftest of the horses in the stable, and was soon headed up the hill toward the Spire. The moon had not yet set, lighting his path so that he did not need a torch, even though dawn was little more than a smudge of grey on the eastern horizon.

By the time he reached the base of the Spire, it was light enough to discern the difference between the tower and the rock behind it. Leaving Pegasus in the pen that held the Spire ponies, he opened the door to the tower.

"Ho, the tower! It's Godfrey, coming up to see the view!"

Male voices urged him to come up. Melisende was likely saving her comments about how unwelcome he was for when he reached the top of the winding stairs, Godfrey thought wryly as he hastened toward the belfry.

Beatus and Clemens offered him a drink from the jug of cider on the table between them, but Melisende was nowhere to be seen.

"Where is she?" Godfrey asked, pouring himself a cup of cider.

"Who?" asked Beatus, tearing his gaze away from the window.

"My sister, Lady Melisende."

The two men stared at one another, confusion clear on their faces.

"She is not here, Sir Godfrey," Clemens said kindly.

Both men had served his father since before he was born, watching him play with a wooden sword before being allowed to trade blows with them in the practice yard. They knew he was slower than his brothers, and their kindness was not condescension.

But he couldn't help clenching his fists in frustration. He felt as stupid as they thought him to be. "But she said she'd be here. Have you seen her tonight?" After a moment, he added, "Or anyone else?"

For if she'd come here to meet a lover, it was not Clemens or Beatus.

Two heads shook. "Not since Firmin and Justus left at sunset, and our watch began."

Godfrey's heart sank. Either he'd been right to worry, or she'd remembered Father's disgust for the crusaders, changed her mind and crept up to bed. No one would have heard her returning home, just as no one would have heard her go if he had not met her on the way. He prayed she was home, asleep, and much wiser than her brother.

He missed his footing more than once on his way down the spiral stair, so he wisely let Pegasus choose her own pace on the steep mountain track. He breathed a sigh of relief when they reached the road, only to be greeted by the daytime guards.

"You need to see this, Sir Godfrey," said Justus, parting the bushes beside the road.

Godfrey swallowed. He prayed he was wrong, before raising his head to look.

A bundle of white wool lay in the bushes, folded in half as though ready to be placed in a chest to be stored for the winter.

Justus nudged the bundle with his foot, rolling it over.

Bile rose up in Godfrey's throat at the ruin of what had once been a human face, but was little more than bloody pulp now. Her gown, and the shift beneath it, were ripped from neck to hem, and so stained in blood one might have thought the cloth was meant to be red.

Justus touched a hand to her throat. "There's no heartbeat. She's dead."

Godfrey nodded, taking in the girl's injuries, for she had no modesty left to preserve. Bleeding out from the vicious cuts to her thighs and belly, she'd crawled into the woods to die after her rape and beating. Another in a long list of victims who could be laid at the crusaders' doors. Sins they would never answer for, if they freed the Holy City.

"Do you recognise her?" Godfrey asked.

Justus coughed. "I'd know that cloak anywhere. 'Tis Lady Melisende, whose stillroom potions kept my mother alive through the winter, when everyone else said she'd never make it."

No. She was asleep in her bed. Home. Safe. Had to be.

"Are you sure?" Godfrey croaked.

The guards exchanged a glance, as if questioning his intelligence. Godfrey had never felt as stupid as he did right now.

"It's the stars embroidered on the hem. When the weather grew warmer, Lady

Melisende forgot her cloak one afternoon, and my mother did the stars as thanks for your sister's care." Justus would not meet Godfrey's eyes. "Would you like help lifting her onto your horse to take home?"

If Godfrey's thoughts had been slow before, they moved at the pace of pitch now. It couldn't be her. Yet it had to be. What he'd dreaded had come to pass, and it was his fault. Now, with her death on his conscience, he would be forced to break the final oath he'd made to her, and tell his father.

It took Godfrey three tries to mount his horse, so Justus and Firmin did not wait for an answer. The two men wrapped the body in the cloak, before passing it up to him. Godfrey couldn't think of the limp bundle as his sister as he rode home with it.

Father sat on the dais in the Great Hall, breaking his fast as he gave orders for the day.

Godfrey's feet kept carrying him forward, though the body in his arms weighed him down so much he feared his next step would send him crashing into the cellar below.

He laid the bundle at the foot of the dais.

"They got Melisende, Father." His throat closed as he choked back a sob. "Those damned crusaders killed her." And I didn't stop them, he thought but did not say. This was his fault. His, and no one else's. "I vow to you, on her soul, that I will seek out the men who did this, and see that they face justice. If I have to follow the army to the gates of the Holy City itself, I will find them, and see that they pay."

Godfrey bowed his head to where the cloak's hood hid his sister's ravaged face, unable to look his father in the eye. "I will pack my things and set off immediately."

He rose and hurried out of the hall. He was a killer and an oathbreaker, no better than any of the crusaders. If he wanted forgiveness for his sins, he would have to not only seek justice for Melisende, but he'd have to see that the crusade succeeded.

He vowed to do everything in his power to ensure no more crusades were needed, so this would never happen again.

Six

"There you are!"

Penelope had barely a moment to register Marzia's presence before the girl grasped Penelope's hand in both of hers and began to pull her toward the convent.

"I've been looking for you everywhere. What possessed you to stand out here in the cold? Why, the breeze blows right through you here – it's a wonder you haven't turned into an icicle. Your hands are colder than the lagoon! I insist you come inside by the fire, before you catch a chill."

Penelope didn't need to glance at the waves to know her father had already vanished from sight, headed home to the much larger islands that made up the main part of the Republic of Rialto. Maybe Marzia's sunny thoughts were exactly the panacea she needed to cure her own dark misgivings.

Penelope allowed herself to be led into the womb-like warmth of the convent parlour, where the more sensible members of the community entertained their guests. Not everyone wore masks for Carnevale – most of the nuns went bare-faced, like Marzia, Penelope and the other…well, Penelope supposed they were officially novices, the girls who were not yet nuns and those who lived within the walls of Saint Angelo of Concordia while they waited to be married.

People parted to allow her passage through the room to the fireplace, where the roaring blaze kept all but the convent dogs at a safe distance.

Marzia produced a sheet of paper and held it out to Penelope. "My brother sent me a letter. Now the mourning period for Father is over, he thinks it is time for me to marry. He says that if his negotiations continue, I will be married by the summer!"

Penelope skimmed the letter, finding nothing new. After Vitale's death, it made sense for his heir to take over his father's role in making a marriage agreement for her. Such was the way of the world. If women were allowed to choose their own husbands, businesses would fail as dowry money went into less suitable hands than those belonging to their fellow merchants, or their sons. Or so many of the men of the city thought.

But she knew Marzia's secret worries about never marrying, now her father was dead. This news was welcome relief for her.

So, "Congratulations. That is good news," Penelope said.

Marzia's eyes shone. "Isn't it? But I must know if I will be happy in marriage. That's why I need you!"

Oh no. Penelope opened her mouth to protest.

"You see, there's a fortune teller," Marzia continued. "She says she can tell my future by merely looking at my hand. But I haven't the courage see her alone. I'm frightened that my future will be dark. If you come with me, to share your fortitude with me, then perhaps I can stand to hear what she has to say."

Penelope followed Marzia's gaze to the old woman seated in a corner of the parlour. At least, that's what she appeared to be. But as Marzia grasped Penelope's hand and led her closer, she began to see the inconsistencies in the woman's costume. Her rags were the remains of several gowns stitched together haphazardly, with little regard for the fine fabric they were made from. The woman's face was a cleverly made Carnivale mask, complete with wrinkles, so that what little she could see of it that wasn't hidden by the hood of her fine wool cloak appeared to be her real face and not artifice. The woman's hand was unusually large, dwarfing the cup in her hand, though most of it was hidden in her voluminous sleeve. Her boots were larger than even the abbess's, and the abbess had big feet for a woman.

Penelope let her mind brush the fortune

teller's thoughts.

"Marzia, what you think is a fortune teller is in fact a fraud. In fact, I think she's a – "

"Some people deny the existence of magic in the world. So caught up in their own business, they think little of the happiness of others. That's why they will always be alone," the old woman croaked sourly, her eyes fixed on Penelope.

Penelope pressed her lips together. A few more words and she might have given away the secret of her gift. Not even her father knew she could read minds, and she had no intention of handing her secret over to this charlatan. A charlatan who knew too much already, to be issuing predictions about her future that seemed likely to come true.

"Not me," Marzia declared, depositing a small pile of silver on the table before the fortune teller. She perched on one end of the bench, pulling Penelope down beside her. "If you can truly tell me my future, I would pay you ten times that."

The greedy glitter Penelope expected in the fortune teller's eyes failed to appear.

"Give me your hand, my little strawberry," the fortune teller said.

Marzia blushed almost as red as her gown, and extended her fingers.

The fortune teller captured her hand like a coveted treasure, cupping it carefully as she turned it palm up. Penelope glimpsed well-manicured nails on distinctly unwrinkled fingers before the fortune teller began to speak.

"This is a happy hand. A very happy hand…"

Had Penelope imagined it, or had the fortune teller's voice grown deeper?

"You will be happily married to a man who will adore you. You will live in a fine house overlooking the campo where his family has lived for generations, and your children – "

"How many children will I have?" Marzia interrupted eagerly.

"As many as you desire, and your husband Marco…"

An overwhelming wave of desire engulfed Penelope, accompanied by the image of a young man entwined with Marzia, naked in a bed of silk. A young man with big hands, big feet, and a huge…

Closing her eyes to shut out the image, Penelope rose and backed away from the fake fortune teller.

Marco of the mighty manhood, she presumed, was now so enamoured of Marzia that he didn't even notice Penelope leaving.

No, not just enamoured – madly in love with her. And who wouldn't be? Penelope's friend was as lovely inside as she was out, and she deserved happiness.

Penelope sighed. If Marzia would have a devoted husband, then perhaps the man was right, and Penelope would spend the rest of her life alone, whether she married or not. For love in marriage was as rare as a flying horse in the merchant city.

Seven

The horde of humanity and horses stretched as far as Godfrey could see. Some had tents or pavilions, while others looked like they'd slept under a hedge and wished they were still there. So much for riding out at dawn. Yesterday's army had become this morning's rabble. Time enough for him to find Melisende's murderers, and bring them before his father to face justice.

"What are you looking for? Did you lose your squire, Sir Knight?"

Godfrey blinked. He hadn't seen the grey-clad man, leaning against a tree beside the road.

"Have you seen anyone else come along this road?" Godfrey demanded.

The grey man pulled a bottle from his belt, yanked out the stopper and drank deeply. He waited until he'd corked the bottle and wiped his mouth on his sleeve before he spoke. "I've seen an entire crusade, Sir Knight. Or did you think magic put all these men here?" He spread his arms wide to encompass the chaos that was the crusader camp.

Godfrey felt his face redden in embarrassment. The grey man must think him a fool, and perhaps he was right. "I mean…since they made camp. Anyone who came this way, leaving the camp, before returning. Likely before dawn."

The grey man nodded, looking thoughtful. "I'll ask you again, Sir Knight. Who are you looking for?"

Godfrey blew out a frustrated breath. "I don't know. I found a girl's body by the road, and I'm looking for the man who killed her."

For a moment, Godfrey thought the grey

man looked relieved, but his expression shifted as quickly as breath in the breeze. Perhaps he had only imagined it.

"You're looking for men with blood on their hands. Take your pick, then, Sir Knight. In this army, there are none without sin. You need but cast the first stone, and you shall surely hit a man who has killed."

Godfrey didn't have time for this. He slid down from his horse and seized the man's shoulder. "Cease your mockery, man. A girl is dead, and she deserves justice. Will you help me, or no?"

The grey man brushed him off, meeting his eyes like a man who knew he was Godfrey's equal. The thickly woven wool beneath Godfrey's hand had told him this was no common labourer.

"If you have any honour, sir, I beg you. Tell me what you know. The girl did not deserve her fate, and honour demands I find the men who deserve death more surely than she did."

The grey man gave a sharp nod. "It's Zoticus, without the sir. I'm no knight, nor do I wish to be. Too much throwing your weight about and riding whatever can carry you, willing or not. The men you want to speak to are the leaders of this rabble, knights all. Sirs Enguerrand, Guiscard, Onfroi and Roland."

Godfrey stepped back. "Thank you, Master Zoticus. Where might I find these knights you have named?"

"Probably asleep in their pavilions, resting after their successful hunt. For if they were awake, the men would be already on the march, obeying the barked orders from their betters." Zoticus cupped a hand to his ear. "Hark, but I do not hear them. Best you leave before you do. Go and see the girl gets a decent burial. You may be sure she died in battle – think of it as an honourable end."

Godfrey shook his head. "She must have justice. I must find the men who did this to her and bring them before my father, so he can judge and punish them for their crimes."

"And what do you think their army will do? At a word from one of these knights, every man among them will fight. Do you have an army that can defeat them?" Zoticus raised his eyebrows. "Are you such a formidable warrior that you could strike all four of them down before they can utter a word?"

Godfrey was under no illusions about his prowess with a sword. He was too slow to be much of a match for anyone. Even Melisende could beat him in the practice ring on occasion, so swift and nimble was she. But if she had not managed to fight her way free from four armed men, Godfrey had no hope.

"I do not fear death, but I cannot die until justice is served." Godfrey moistened his lips. "There must be a way."

Zoticus winked. "Oh, there is, Sir Knight. But you might not think it honourable for such a noble knight like yourself."

He closed his eyes. "I seek justice, for I have no honour to speak of until she is avenged." Godfrey swallowed. "How can I make them pay for what they have done?"

Zoticus lowered his voice. "Even the most combat hardened knight cannot defend against everything in the heat of battle. Especially the blow that comes from an ally. No one need ever know the enemy blow was struck from within their own ranks. And in battle, each knight leads his own men – they will not know the fate of the others until the battle is over."

Godfrey stared at him, trying to puzzle out all possible meanings of the grey man's words. "You mean…I should befriend them, ride with them, until we ride into battle against the unbelievers…and then assassinate them?" Hardly honourable, but then whoever had killed Melisende had no honour, either. They were all damned together, but it would all be for Melisende. Unless this man was lying and he or someone else had killed his sister… "What if it wasn't them?" he blurted out.

Zoticus smiled, but the expression seemed as grim and grey as his tunic. "It will be many months before we reach the Holy Land, and maybe even longer before the first battle begins. If you ride with us, you will soon see what sort of men they are."

Godfrey nodded. From what little he knew of him, Zoticus gave sound advice. Though the grey man could not be more than a few years older than Godfrey himself.

"Good," Zoticus said. "When battle begins, I shall find you. Enguerrand and Roland are mean fighters, and you might have need of another blade to help you in your quest." He held out his arm, one warrior offering assistance to another.

Godfrey clasped it. "Thank you, Master Zoticus." He rode on, through the camp.

It wasn't until he was deep among the crusaders that he realised Zoticus' plan was far too detailed for something he'd thought up in the moments since they'd met. In fact, it sounded like something he'd been planning for some time.

Zoticus had some stake here, too, which he had not chosen to share.

It mattered not. The men who had killed Melisende would pay for it, and that was enough for Godfrey. If they paid for their other crimes, too, for surely they had committed many, then he was the last man to protest against such justice.

The crusade would be long enough for Godfrey to take the measure of more than one man along the way.

Eight

Cloudy skies turned the lagoon waters iron grey, as if to armour the waves against the pelting rain. The weather's war kept most visitors away from the convent, but the clouds and the waves reached a stalemate eventually, as they always did, and some brave boats ventured out again.

Penelope heard their thoughts as first the fishermen, then the merchants with supplies for the outer islands rowed past. Their prayers for profit and a safe voyage were little more than a hum in the back of her mind, as she worked with her loom. She had finished Marzia's wedding dress before the year ended, but now she fancied making a veil to match. It would use the last of the blue wool, too, from that peculiar dye batch that was precisely the colour of Vitale's family coat of arms. It brought out the colour of Marzia's eyes, too.

Not for the first time, she blessed her father's gift of horn shutters for the workroom windows here at Saint Angelo's. They let in enough light to allow her to work despite the dark day, yet kept the swift wind from stealing away the heat of her fire. If the light held, she might finish weaving the cloth today, so that she could start sewing the veil before night fell.

Something metal clattered to the table behind her and Penelope jumped to her feet.

"You missed dinner again," Marzia greeted her, folding her arms across her chest. "So I brought you some."

Penelope glanced at the plate. Dinnertime already? She had not eaten since breakfast, and it took a moment to register that she was hungry.

"But the cloth for your wedding veil has

come out so perfectly. I wanted to do it all in one piece..." Penelope waved at the sea of blue on her loom.

Marzia looked longingly at the cloth. "For me? Oh, it is so pretty. But how could you know?"

Marzia was practically bursting to tell Penelope her news. She must have truly been caught up in her work not to have noticed the thoughts screaming to be heard from Marzia's mind.

Penelope shook her head, hoping to clear it. "What news?" she asked, feigning ignorance.

Marzia clapped her hands. "Oh, you will never believe it. My brother came to visit me today, and with him he brought...my betrothed! A handsome young nobleman called Marco, just like the fortune teller predicted! He had been intended for the church, but after his father and brothers died in battle under Father's command, he was forced to take over the family business and to find a wife. He did not wish to marry Father's daughter, after what happened, but my brother persuaded him to come here to meet me, and…oh, you won't believe it. The moment he saw me he fell in love!"

At least Marco the fake fortune teller hadn't lied about that. Perhaps there'd been a little more lust than love, but there was nothing wrong with a man lusting after his wife.

And when that wife was Marzia…

"Of course he did," Penelope said, moving from her loom to the chest by the window. "So it's probably past time I gave you this…" She opened the chest and lifted out the blue gown she'd spent most of the winter working on. "It's a bit plain, but as you're so much better at embroidery than me, I thought you'd prefer to do the fine work yourself, or at least tell me what you want so I can attempt it."

Marzia's eyes shone with tears as her shaking hands reached for the gown. "It's beautiful. I've never seen any cloth so blue. Except for the silk scarf you gave me at Christmas…"

Cut from the same cloth as the gown. "Let's see how well it fits," Penelope suggested. Not bothering to summon a maid, Penelope helped her friend out of her overdress and into the blue gown. She laced it up with eager efficiency, wanting to see if she'd judged the cut correctly. With Marzia's small breasts, cutting it too low in the front would expose far too much flesh. As it was…perhaps a ribbon across the neckline in white or silver would help.

"Can I see?" Marzia asked.

Penelope blinked, annoyed at herself for not thinking. She lifted her hand mirror out of the chest and angled it so that Marzia might see what she looked like.

"It's perfect!" Marzia breathed.

"I thought it would make a lovely wedding dress," Penelope said carefully, tweaking the skirt so it caught the light just right. "Along with the veil."

Marzia's face fell. "Oh, it would, but Marco's family are prolific lace makers, and his family's wedding gift to me is an entire chest of lace. If I don't wear it to the wedding, it would be a terrible insult to his mother and sisters, and they would hate me. I could not bear it if —
"

"What colour is the lace?" Penelope

interrupted.

"Like fresh cream. I confess that when he first opened the chest, I thought I was looking at a cake," Marzia said with a laugh.

A little at the neckline, perhaps at the sleeves and at the hem, and if there was enough, edging the veil, too…Marzia would not need embroidery, with lace edging her gown. If there was enough lace, perhaps she could lay it over the veil, letting the blue peep through the design…

"Can you show me?" Penelope asked.

"Yes, it's in my sleeping chamber. But you'll have to come with me, for the chest is so large I cannot hope to lift it." Marzia extended a hand.

Penelope took it, letting her friend pull her out of the workroom to where she kept a king's ransom in lace.

Yard after yard of the stuff, enough to edge this gown and make another one entirely. Or…

Penelope lifted an armload of the linen cut-work lace and offered a prayer of thanks for the talent of Marco's mother as she draped it over Marzia's head. "How about a veil of trailing lace, cut like a cloak, so that it fans out behind you when you walk, but pinned open here and here…"

Between Marzia's shining eyes and her own rising satisfaction, Penelope was soon so wrapped up in her work she had no need to worry about suitors or marriage or anything in her own future. Her thoughts and her hands were filled with the most beautiful wedding gown Rialto nobility had ever seen, on the sweetest bride any man could ever marry.

Nine

Godfrey woke with a groan, his head throbbing like someone had cleaved it in two. If they hadn't, he wished they would, so it would stop hurting so. But there'd been a girl, her clothes so full of holes you could see her skin beneath, blue from cold in the night air, her eyes enormous with fear as Sir Enguerrand and his Unholy Trinity of bastards as cruel as he was encircled her. Her clothes had likely been perfectly serviceable before one of them (Sir Roland, most likely) had tried to grab her and the cloth had torn as she'd tried to get away.

By the time he'd arrived, the knights had starting tearing her clothing away in tiny pieces, not caring when their blades nicked flesh.

Godfrey had downed Guiscard with one punch, but then Enguerrand and Onfroi had been upon him, and Roland had vanished. Godfrey had seen Roland again for barely a moment before blackness had engulfed him.

Now, there was no sign of the four men, or the girl. If scraps of cloth had not still littered the ground, he might have wished it was nothing but a bad dream. If the girl's body wasn't sharing the alley with him, perhaps she'd gotten away.

He tried to sit up and groaned again as a spike of pain blurred his vision and threatened to send him back into oblivion.

It took him an embarrassingly long time to get to his feet — after he'd voided the contents of his stomach — so that he might stagger out of the shadows into the light. He made it three steps before he slipped in a puddle of something foul-smelling and went down again amid a pile of refuse.

If he'd thought the girl's eyes were wide and terrified before…they bulged almost out of her head now.

And the stench…

Godfrey vomited again, turning his head so that he wouldn't desecrate her corpse any more than he had already. The poor girl had not deserved this fate, any more than Melisende had.

He'd failed them both.

Digging his fingers into the mortar of the wall beside him, Godfrey heaved himself to his feet. Now, he had to find his way back to the inn where he'd left his belongings.

The bustle of Byzas went on around him as Godfrey trudged along the streets, shading his eyes against the painfully bright light that reflected off everything. What had possessed these people to build a city of red and white bricks, or sheathe any of the walls in marble? Oh, what he would give for the familiar dark timbers and stones of home!

But home was an inn, at least until he'd succeeded in his personal crusade to satisfy poor Melisende's honour.

At least it was darker inside the inn, where he asked for a headache draught and a jug of water to be sent up to his room as he made his laborious way up the stairs.

When the potion arrived, he drank it, then washed it down with a cup of weak ale, before washing off the filth from the alley.

"Would you like more water, sir?" the serving girl asked.

Godfrey looked up, surprised to see the servant had stayed. She'd been quick bringing the potion, too. Unlike when he'd arrived, when it had taken half a day before any water had been sent up. The inn had been full of crusaders, and so busy that on his first night here, he'd woken a dozen times to the incessant sound of pounding feet on the stairs from servants and guests alike.

The stairs were silent now, and it appeared the servants had time to stand and wait.

Godfrey swallowed. "Have the army left?"

Her head bobbed. "Yes, sir. They left three days ago."

Three days? He'd been unconscious that

long? No wonder the girl's corpse had smelled so awful. She'd been dead for three days or more.

He had no time to waste. "No, I won't be needing anything else, except for someone to saddle my horse."

"Yes, sir." The servant curtseyed and left.

Godfrey stripped off his filthy clothes and donned a fresh set, then buckled on his leather armour. If he had to ride fast through lands the army had already raped, there would likely be plenty of unhappy inhabitants only too happy to attack a lone knight who'd fallen behind.

Ten

Godfrey reached the inn yard before his horse. Perhaps the maid had forgotten to relay his request to the grooms, or been waylaid, he told himself. Or the stablehands were lazy.

At home, neither he or his father would stand for such sloth from stablehands. After paying more than a stablehand's monthly wages to the inn to keep his horse for the few days he was in the city, Godfrey had no intention of tolerating slothfulness here. Especially when every moment counted, if he wanted to catch up to the army again.

"Ho, the stables!" he shouted, then winced as the sound seemed to ring in his still tender head. The potion wasn't working properly yet. He repeated his greeting, a little more quietly, as he crossed the threshold.

He'd never entered a stable so silent, except when the horses were all out in the fields. But even then, the stablehands would be mucking out the stalls, filling the stable with the sounds of scraping shovels and swishing brooms. A quick peek into the first stall told him why — there was nothing but fresh straw and water. Every stall was the same, from one end of the cavernous stable to the other.

No wonder his horse wasn't saddled and ready for him, if they'd had to retrieve Pegasus from some field outside the city. Perhaps it would be faster for him to go to Pegasus.

A brief search revealed the grooms sharing a jug of ale outside the kitchen door.

"Where is my horse? A silver coin to the man who can take me to him," Godfrey said, holding up the coin.

The men looked at one another, before a boy blurted out, "But sir, there are no horses here. No horses for nigh on three days. 'Tis like a holiday, blessing us for taking such good care of the holy crusader knights!"

"More like the devil has tempted you into laziness, for I am a knight, and without my horse, I shall not be able to reach the Holy Land," Godfrey said grimly. "I left her here, in your care. I would have returned sooner, but some rogue set upon me in an alley, attacking me from behind, and left me for dead. Now I have returned, I need my horse to rejoin the army." Or Melisende's honour was dead, along with his. It was worse than Rialto – would his bad luck never end?

"What did your horse look like, Sir Knight?" one of the older grooms ventured. "We do not have your horse, but maybe we can tell you who stole him."

"Her," Godfrey corrected. "Pegasus would have been the finest horse in your stable. Perhaps the finest horse you have ever seen, for not even the Emperor has one of our horses yet. She is grey, so pale you might think she was white, and as fast as the wind when she begins to run. Why, a man lucky enough to ride a mare like her might think he was flying."

The groom paled, and muttered swearing came from the others. "A pale grey mare, you say? Such a rare beast was in the stables until three days ago, when Sir Roland insisted she be saddled for the journey. There was a loud argument in the square between Sir Roland and Sir Enguerrand over who owned the horse as right of conquest, or some such knightly thing. Swords were drawn, and there was quite the battle between the two men before Sir Enguerrand won the victory, and left upon the grey horse. Sir Roland was wounded, but he rode out an hour later, on another, lesser beast."

Did none of them have a shred of honour between them? To leave a fellow knight unconscious in an alley, then steal his horse...even if Melisende were still at home safe, Enguerrand and his pack of rogues would deserve to die. Now...he swore that Enguerrand and Roland would be the first to taste his blade.

But in order to do that...he would need to catch them first. And in order to catch them, he would need a horse as swift as Pegasus.

"I need a horse. Not any old nag, but one that can run all day without tiring, and wake the next day to do it again. One that will take me to the army, and the men who stole from me."

Another groom shook his head. "You will find no such horse in the city. The crusader knights bought every horse they could find, and even a few lame donkeys. The only mounts left in the city are children's toys."

"Or the ones in the Emperor's stable," the boy piped up. "I heard he posted extra guards to keep the army out. My brother's a guard at the palace, and he said –"

One of the older men hushed him, but not before Godfrey had time to think it sounded much like the guards they'd set on his own stables at home. And if the Emperor did not yet have one of his family's horses…perhaps he would like to. In exchange for the loan of one of his own…

Any other time, it was the sort of bargain Godfrey could never consider, but with Melisende's honour at stake…a horse was a small price to pay. Even Pegasus.

Godfrey flipped the coin to the boy. "To buy you all another drink, in thanks for your help, if you will all swear to it that the fight between Roland and Enguerrand was over my stolen horse."

The men swiftly swore that they had witnessed the events themselves, just as the first man had told it.

Godfrey nodded, then headed for the palace, and his only chance to make good on his vow. He might not be the best fighter, but he knew the horse trade. All he had to do was convince the Emperor to part with the best horse in his stable…in trade for a far superior animal when Godfrey returned.

Simple, surely.

Eleven

Even without the dress, Marzia would have been the most beautiful bride the people of Rialto had ever seen. Glowing with love for her groom, her face rivalled the sun itself, surrounded by a firmament of lace clouds upon a dreamy blue sky.

If Penelope was even half as happy on her own wedding day, she would consider herself blessed indeed.

Marzia grasped Penelope's hands and refused to board her gondola unless her friend came with her. "I'm so nervous!" the girl said.

"What if he changes his mind and doesn't want to marry me? What if..."

Penelope spent most of the trip across the lagoon soothing Marzia's fears, which didn't fade until she spotted Marco outside the church. Marco's thoughts were so loud, Penelope could hear him clear across the campo, before they'd even docked.

The man vowed he would kill anyone who came between him and Marzia, and that death would be slow and torturous should anyone try to take his bride away from him. She was his, and tonight he was going to...

Penelope bit down hard on her lip, willing the magic in her veins to silence her gift, if only for a little while, so she did not see Marco's plans for his bride in their bedchamber tonight. By the time her lip stopped bleeding, they were inside the church and listening to the priest perform the marriage ceremony. Luckily, most of the people present were thinking about their own weddings, whether in the past or the future, if they weren't listening to the priest.

Sometimes her gift was a blessing, but at

other times, it seemed more of a curse. Most other witches paid a blood price to cast their spells or use their talents, while her gift let her listen to others' thoughts until she paid a blood price to stop it, a sweet silence that never lasted long enough.

But now…her father's thoughts wandered from the wedding to her, and what her future might hold. Aachen, Byzas, or some merchant prince here at home? He kept returning to Prince Alexios of Byzas, because an alliance between the Emperor of Byzas and the Duke of Rialto might free the Rialtine prisoners the Emperor held in his dungeons, even now. But with Prince Otto's father so rich, he would take her without a dowry, which he might have to, given what foolishness her brothers had invested it in.

Penelope blinked. She'd known her father had set aside a substantial dowry for her, and she'd also known about her brothers' northern expedition. Orso's idea, she knew, but only now did she realise that Pietro had persuaded her father to take her dowry money to finance it, and now they'd lost it all. Instead of bringing home expensive furs from the icy northern wastes, the ships had been taken by pirates, never to be seen again.

So she might not marry at all, or be forced to go north to Aachen, and never see the waters of home again.

Because the merchant prince her father had in mind for her had been Marco, if the man had rejected Marzia the way everyone had expected. Except…Marco was very much a man in love, kissing his bride so tenderly more than one girl thought she might swoon.

Otto or Alexios, then, Penelope told herself. Or no one at all.

Bleakness opened up a terrible, aching hole in her heart. Penelope would be alone all her life, and the sort of love radiating out of Marco and Marzia was something she would never know.

Oh, what a miserable thought. She should be ashamed of herself, thinking such maudlin things on this joyous day.

Perhaps that was why her gift was so arse-about, compared to everyone else. Instead of silencing the joy and fond memories around her, she opened herself to them, pouring that shared joy into the void she had no need to feel.

Today, her friend married the man she loved, a man who loved her more than anyone else in the world. Tonight, in the privacy of her bed, Penelope might mourn, if she wished, that she would never find such happiness. Few people would, so to see it before her now…it warmed her heart.

And whether she went to Byzas or Aachen or anywhere, she would keep the memory of this day close. Because if her father married her off for a foreign alliance, he did so to keep Marzia and all the other girls like her safe.

Men went away to fight   how would her fate be any different? Penelope had no right to be a coward, when the price of her sacrifice might be lasting peace.

As long as she had all she needed to turn simple thread into clothing that earned its wearer the kind of envy Marzia garnered today, she could make a life anywhere.

Twelve

Godfrey eyed the long line of petitioners before him and swallowed. They stretched the length of the enormous throne room and down the steps to the square outside. He'd be lucky to enter the throne room today, let alone speak to Emperor Manuel.

But what other choice did he have?

He settled in for a long wait.

Climbing the stairs took an hour, and when he reached the throne room, he realised why. Petitioners were heard by a row of men who stood at the base of the dais where the

Emperor's throne sat. The Emperor himself looked half asleep, stirring only to wave an indolent hand when one of the men addressed him. No matter what the verdict was, a number of guards would surround the petitioner, who either strode off with them in a sort of stunned disbelief, or screamed and fought while the guards carried him away.

"The previous emperor ordered his own brother's eyes to be plucked out when he offended him. Hell might be preferable to the things that go on in these dungeons," the man in front of Godfrey whispered to his companion.

Godfrey uttered a silent prayer that his petition would not see him sent to the Emperor's dungeons.

"The last petitioner that His Imperial Majesty will hear today, Lord Valerio of Rialto," the herald announced.

Godfrey's heart sank. If he didn't get a horse from the Emperor today, he'd never catch up to the army. Shoulders slumped, he turned to leave the throne room.

A voice boomed out, louder than even the

herald: "Your Imperial Majesty, lords and ladies of the court, I am Lord Valerio of Rialto, a magician of great power, and I call on all of you to bear witness to my pledge to use my powers in service of His Imperial Majesty, Emperor Manuel!"

Silence fell across the room as everyone turned to see the magician.

Even Godfrey paused on the threshold to listen, the crowd was too thick for him to see the Rialto magician.

But he did see the Emperor wake from his torpor. "What manner of magic?" the Emperor rumbled.

"The power of flight!"

Murmurings and whisperings swept through the room, as every man asked his neighbour whether they had heard true.

"Show me," the Emperor demanded, rising to his feet.

"The enchanted beast is in the square outside, and I will be only too happy to give Your Imperial Majesty a demonstration," Lord Valerio said.

The crowd parted and Godfrey glimpsed a

man in Rialto style robes hurrying toward him, the Emperor striding behind.

Godfrey slipped out the door, setting his back to the wall at the top of the steps, staying out of the way whilst making sure he could see what happened next.

The magician trotted down the steps, stopping when he reached a crude wooden statue of a horse. He spread his arms wide. "Behold, the legendary enchanted horse, destroyer of cities, since an ancient wizard, my ancestor, first constructed it to bring about the fall of ancient Ilium!"

Several people in the square tittered at this impossible claim. The thing barely looked like a horse, and even Godfrey knew it could not be the horse that brought about Ilium's doom. The horse of legend had carried troops secretly into the city, so that they might open the gates to let the invading army in. This wooden thing, though it might be the size of a real horse, didn't look like it could fit a single man inside it.

The fake magician was destined for the dungeons, Godfrey was sure of it.

As if reading his thoughts, a squad of guards approached the man and his crude horse.

"Allow me to show you its power!" the magician said, leaping upon the horse's back.

All right, it could carry one man, maybe two, like that, but still there was the matter of it moving…

The magician leaned over the horse's neck to touch the place where a bridle might go on a real horse.

Screams erupted from the crowd. It took Godfrey a moment to see why – the horse's hooves had risen from the ground to stand on nothing but air, and still the thing lifted higher.

"Behold, the enchanted horse!" the magician roared as he rose level with the steps, then the roof, and up into the air itself.

Godfrey couldn't seem to close his mouth. It was magic – it had to be. However crude its appearance, a flying horse could indeed sneak men into a city. Free as a bird, they could simply fly over the mighty walls, for Ilium's walls had been legend, surpassed only by the ramparts encircling Byzas today. Anyone who possessed the such a horse could come and go as they pleased, armies and walls notwithstanding. The man who owned it would be unstoppable.

When the magician and his horse landed on the ground, the Emperor himself stepped through the doors to stand on the top step, only a few yards from Godfrey. Godfrey held his breath, not daring to move. Guards held the crowd back both inside and out, yet in his spot, half-hidden by the throne room doors, he'd gone unnoticed. If he could keep it that way just a little longer…

"Give me that horse," the Emperor demanded.

For a moment, Godfrey was reminded of his toddler nephew, from the Emperor's tone right down to his reaching hand. A comical thing to see, from a man old enough to be his father, yet no one laughed.

The magician smiled as he dismounted, then bowed fussily at the Emperor's feet. "I would gladly make it my gift to you, Your Imperial Majesty, but to part with such a precious family heirloom…I would be a fool indeed. But I might be willing to trade for it…"

"What do you want?"

There was no trace of the toddler now — something in the Emperor's tone sent a shiver down Godfrey's spine. This was a man who liked torture.

A man who would never trade for something he might simply take.

Somehow, the magician missed the danger. "I would not part with a family heirloom to anyone who is not family. But if you were to give me your daughter to be my wife, this grateful groom might be willing to give this priceless horse as a gift to his father-in-law."

The Emperor spluttered, then recovered so quickly Godfrey thought he'd imagined it. "Take the impudent wretch to the dungeons," the Emperor said.

No less than six guards closed in on the magician, seizing him before he could return to his horse. They started to carry him away.

"Any man who touches that horse who is not part of my family will suffer the most terrible curse. Him, and every descendant fate allows the misfortune of being born in his bloodline!" the magician howled.

The crowd edged away from the horse.

"Put the horse in my stable," the Emperor ordered.

The remaining guards didn't move.

"Is no man brave enough to touch that hunk of wood? It's not even a real horse — it's not like it can bite!" the Emperor said. "Surely someone can ride it."

Against all odds, the Emperor himself was offering the only horse who might be able to catch the crusaders.

Madness made the decision for him.

"I can," Godfrey said. "I am Sir Godfrey of Maraschal. My father's barony is home to the greatest horses in the world. I have never met a horse I could not handle, and this will not be the first." He reached the bottom of the steps, then turned and bowed deeply to the Emperor. "At your service, Your Imperial Majesty."

"Very well, Sir Knight. Show us your prowess."

Praying that his momentary madness would not get him killed or cursed, Godfrey forced himself to head toward the horse. There were no stirrups or saddle, but a faint indentation where a stirrup might have hung was enough to help him onto the horse's back. The wood had been rubbed smooth by age or countless riders, but he could still faintly see that the horse had originally been more life-like. Now, the ears were worn down to mere nubs, and the carved mane was all but invisible to all but his probing fingers as he sought whatever the magician had touched on the horse's neck to make it fly.

Nothing…nothing but worn wood, and the increasingly impatient Emperor, about to order his guards to take Godfrey to the dungeons, too.

Godfrey wished he'd had time to win back Melisende's honour. To bring justice to the men who had killed her and stolen his horse, and to complete the crusade that would save his soul and the Holy Land, too. If he could have done all that, then maybe he could have returned to Rialto, to resume trade with Lord Sebastiano, and see his enchanting daughter one more time…

Lady Penelope. He breathed her name like a prayer as the image of her angelic face filled his mind. Then his probing fingers touched something sharp and metallic hidden at the horse's throat, drawing blood as he yelped in pain.

Shouts rose up around him, but the sound faded as he focussed on his last memory of Lady Penelope. If he was to die today, he would die dreaming of her.

Thirteen

Fat Tuesday, the final day of Carnevale, and for the first time, Penelope fully felt the weight of the day. Oh, not its religious significance — nothing so spiritual. No, she felt full to bursting from Marzia and Marco's wedding feast. Glutted on good spirits, she didn't dare drink another cup of wine, lest she lose her wits entirely.

She should return to the convent. A short voyage on the lagoon with the ocean breeze should clear her head. No one would notice her absence. Not even…

Marzia beamed at her. "Are you ready for the trial? My Marco insists we must all go to the Campo San Marco to see the pigs and bulls on trial, before they are executed, and stay for the feast."

The trial was a strange ritual that had begun during Duke Vitale's rule, where a bishop who had raided and looted some Rialto churches was required to make annual reparation – a bull and a dozen pigs, representing himself and his priests, which were subjected to a criminal trial, convicted and then executed by a mob of the people of Rialto. The slaughtered beasts were then roasted and eaten on the spot.

Penelope had witnessed one such trial, and never wanted to see another. Normal people's thoughts turned savage, intent on capturing and killing the pigs as they ran about in a panic all around the campo. If she attended the trial today, she would likely vomit up every bite she'd eaten since breakfast.

"Come, we must get to the boats!" Marzia said.

Marco seized her around the waist and carried her to a gondola, ordering the boatman to make haste. Even as the boat headed away, Marzia beckoned Penelope to follow.

Shaking her head, Penelope found a boat willing to take her home to Saint Angelo.

For the duration of the trip, she breathed in the clean, salt air, and wished her friend a happy and fruitful marriage.

Sooner than she expected, she stepped ashore at Saint Angelo, paid the boatman, and headed inside.

Blessed quiet enveloped her as the empty convent closed around her. On this last day of indulgence, even the nuns were spending time with their families, preparing for the fast to come on the morrow.

Penelope, however, had indulged enough. She unfastened her cloak as she headed for her chamber, where she might lie down, just for a moment.

The moment her head touched the pillow, sleep claimed her for its own.

Fourteen

The sounds of the crowd had grown so faint, it was as though they'd vanished entirely. Or maybe it was the rushing in his ears, blocking out all other sound. The pain potion had worn off, and Godfrey's head had begun throbbing again. This pain was nothing compared to that which would be inflicted by the Emperor's torturers when he reached the dungeon.

Any moment now, the guards would reach him, pull him off the stupid wooden horse and drag him down to the dungeons. Any moment now…

But the moment did not come.

Godfrey dared to open his eyes. Then squeezed them shut again, praying his eyes were lying to him.

Slowly, he opened them once more.

Mist enveloped him, strange strands that hid both the earth and sky from him, not to mention the crowd and the guards. Then the mist ended, and his breath left him in a panicked shout. Godfrey clung to the horse's neck as if his life depended on it.

For surely it did, floating so high up he could scarcely see the ground. If he lost his grip on the horse, the fall would surely kill him. Below him, the city had gone, to be replaced with ploughed fields ready to bear this year's crops. He was flying.

Godfrey sucked a breath into his starved lungs, then another. A cloudbank loomed ahead of him, and he watched in wonder as it enveloped him like wet fleece, soaking him to the skin. He'd always imagined clouds as fine, fluffy things that would feel like lambswool, but the reality was far more chilling, like bathing in the rain.

When moisture started dripping down his back, he pulled on his helm in the hope that some of the water would roll off it instead of under his tunic. Hunching against the horse's neck, he peered below. The cloud thinned occasionally, giving him a glimpse of fields and a small town, but not the city of Byzas or any sign of the crusading army.

He was a fool, far more foolish than the magician who had brought his enchanted horse to court. Godfrey should never have risen to the Emperor's mad challenge. Instead, he should have headed home, to beg his father's forgiveness for yet another failure. Then settled into his life at home, taking care of the horses.

Never to leave his father's estate. Never to see Lady Penelope again…

Did he imagine it, or did the horse speed up?

No, he must be imagining it. The beast's wooden legs didn't move. It had but one speed, at which it floated through clouds and open sky, taking him to destinations unknown.

Where a worse fate likely awaited him than

spending his final days in the Emperor's dungeons.

Godfrey sighed and hung on.

Fifteen

Alone, now and forever, just like Marco had said.

The horrible thought jolted Penelope awake, and no matter how much she tried to, she could not shake it. She was alone at Saint Angelo, and she would be until the nuns returned in the morning. She reached out for the comforting thoughts of someone, anyone, even a fisherman late out on the lagoon.

A screech of outrage and an angry image of something in the sky was the first thing she found.

Penelope almost laughed. No, she was not alone. The abbess had left her monkey here in its cage, where the beast raged at its sworn enemy, a sea eagle who nested on the sandbank off the end of the island. If she strained her ears, she thought she heard the eagle's answering shriek.

As long as she lived on Saint Angelo, she would never be alone.

While she'd slept, darkness had fallen, so she lit a candle and carried it down to the kitchen. With a day of fasting tomorrow, there was no need for the cook to set bread to rising, but the smell of old yeast haunted the room, reminding her that she'd missed dinner.

Penelope headed to the buttery, where the morning's milk stood in pails, the cream floating on top, waiting to be made into cheese on the morrow. She drank a cup, then ladled another to take back to the kitchen with her.

She sliced up a spiced sausage – likely the last she would taste until Easter – and found some of the morning's bread and a dish of oil to dip it in. It would do.

She finished her supper, then washed it all

down with a third cup of milk. Anything but wine.

Full and yawning, she headed back to bed.

Sixteen

A chill had settled into Godfrey's bones, yet still the horse flew, showing no signs of stopping. The sinking sun sent a shiver of alarm through him – without the sun to warm him, he might freeze to death. But he could neither stop the sun nor land the horse, so on he flew, growing colder and colder, as his mind grew more and more sluggish.

He thought he smelled the salt of the sea, but he could not be certain. Perhaps he had only dreamed it. Like he'd dreamed a fire, and a hot meal, and a soft bed instead of the hard horse beneath him.

A seabird's shriek penetrated his doze. No, not a seabird – it sounded more like an eagle than a gull. An eagle deprived of its kill, like when a shepherd saved a lamb.

But there was that sibilant sound behind it, like the river rushing past, or waves breaking on a beach. The bird shrieked again, answered by the almost human screech of what could only be a monkey. For no human could make such a sound, unless they were rendered so insensible from pain that they forgot whatever words they might once have known.

The horse bumped against something, a jolt Godfrey felt through his bones. He lost his grip on the horse's neck and felt himself sliding, sliding…toward his death far below.

He scrabbled for a handhold, but the smooth wood slipped beneath his fingers, slick from all the clouds he'd passed through, and he was falling, falling…

The impact knocked the breath from him. For a moment, Godfrey thought he was dead, but air ripped into his lungs and he felt grass between his fingers. The wind down here had not lessened. If anything, it had grown stronger, making him wish more than ever that he'd brought a heavy cloak with him.

He crawled blindly in the dark until he found a spot where the wind could not reach him. There, he curled up and drifted off into an uneasy sleep.

<h1 style="text-align:center">Seventeen</h1>

The sky had barely begun to lighten in warning of the coming dawn when the abbess's monkey started screeching again. Swearing softly, Penelope rose. She eyed the hearth, where a fire was laid, ready to light, but that would take too much time. Instead, she donned her thickest hose inside her fleece-lined boots, wrapped a cloak over her woollen dress, and headed out into the orchard.

At least she'd remembered her gloves this morning, she thought, as frost crunched beneath her boots. The orange trees glowed in the first rays of dawn, placed as they were on the south east corner of the island. A good thing, too, for she hadn't brought a lantern. She filled a basket with ripe oranges, and brought it to the monkey cage. The creature was a Barbary ape, the abbess had told her, brought by ship from the lands far to the west, and it only slept in the cage when the abbess was away. The abbess called it Paz, for the golden colour of its fur, and it was fond of fruit.

This was the first time Penelope had ventured close enough to call it anything, or to feed it, but she cut an orange in half and held it out to the creature. Paz snatched up the orange in one hand, but it kept pointing with the other as it screeched even louder.

Penelope followed the direction of its pointing finger, weaving between the trees and shrubs until she reached the edge of the orchard.

Sure enough, she spotted the sea eagle, perched at the ape's eye level, when he sat in his cage overlooking the trees. But only as she rounded the last berry bush did she fully appreciate the bird's new perch. It looked like a giant flotsam horse, thrown up by the tide to stand upright on the grass. Its time in the water had worn it smooth, so the oak it must have originally been made of had turned shiny black. How long had it drifted, riding the waves, until it made landfall here at Saint Angelo?

She stepped forward to lay her hand on the horse's nose, and the eagle took flight with an affronted shriek, which the monkey drowned out with a rant of its own.

Magic moved beneath her hand, coursing through the horse like blood. Someone particularly powerful had crafted the creature, which must have been almost lifelike before the sea had claimed it. Yet the magic remained, thrumming with more power than she possessed. She bit her lip, concentrating on the magic. The spells upon it had been cast by an enchanter, a man who had fought in many battles, with both wits and sword, who wanted…an end to war. A home, a family. A much-loved wife. The longing was so strong she could almost taste it, though the man was not here.

She took her hands off the horse, yet the ghost of longing remained. Almost as if the man was a ghost himself now.

She sighed, and became aware of the monkey, now punctuating its screeching by banging on the bars of its cage. Hungry for another orange, most likely. She picked up the basket and headed back to the cage.

An armoured man stood beside the bars, staring at the monkey.

Penelope hefted the orange, assessing its weight. She'd thrown stones at gulls as a child, to scare them away from the fishermen's catch, and her aim had been true. An orange might not do more than bruise the man, but it was all she had.

"Step away from the monkey. The abbess does not take kindly to thieves, or men who come to Saint Angelo uninvited," Penelope warned.

The knight whirled, his eyes dark pools within his helm. Pools that she could not read. Nor his thoughts, which were a whirl of confusion still fogged by sleep.

He held up his hands as if in surrender.

Some knight, if he feared a woman.

But no, there was no fear in his mind. Some pain from a long ride, dread of disappointing some ruler, all wrapped in that confusing fog.

"Who are you, and what is your business here?" Penelope demanded. A girl might never rule Rialto, but she knew the effect of an imperious manner, and she had learned from the best.

"I am…I am…I don't know where I am. There was a horse…"

She jerked her head toward the beach. "You mean the wooden one? With magic?"

"An enchanted horse…" he muttered, pulling off his helm as he shambled toward her. No, toward the horse, she realised as he headed past her without pausing.

"You didn't answer my question!" she shouted after him. When he ignored her, she threw the orange at his back.

It hit with a satisfying smack between his shoulder blades. He turned, or tried to, getting his legs so tangled that they tripped him. He landed on his face and didn't rise.

Swearing again, Penelope approached him, confident that she would hear any threats in his thoughts before he had time to act. He was well muscled from his knightly training, or whatever it was that such men did. He had the strength to overpower her, if he wished. But right now, his thoughts were not of violence at all. If anything, he wanted to curl up and sleep.

"You can sleep later. Perhaps the nuns will treat whatever wounds you have. But first, you must answer my questions. Now, get up!"

He merely groaned. Not good.

She knelt beside him and shoved until she rolled him onto his side, then his back. The hood of her cloak came off, letting the wind play with her hair, but she ignored it, focussing instead on the injured man before her.

His eyes met hers and the recognition was mutual.

"Lady Penelope?"

"Godfrey?"

Eighteen

Godfrey managed a sickly smile. Even that hurt. "It's Sir Godfrey now," he said. As if it mattered. Knight or not, he would never be good enough for her.

She grimaced. "So I see. Where are your wounds?" She surveyed his body, then looked thoughtful. "Turn over, so I can see your…back." She blushed.

She knew his arse hurt from riding that horrible horse. A magical horse she'd recognised as such. Godfrey felt his own face grow red. "You truly do read minds."

She reared back, moving away from him. "Don't be silly. No one can do that."

"Not without magic, they can't," he persisted. "That's how you do it, isn't it? It's magic."

She stopped dead and turned to face him. There wasn't a shadow of fear in her expression as she hissed, "If you so much as think to breathe a word of this to anyone, I will cast a curse on you so cruel you will wish you were dead."

He almost laughed. "That's what the other guy said he'd do if I touched his horse. Yet here I am."

She thrust a finger at the horse. "You stole that horse from the sorcerer who made it?" All colour drained from her face. "You have to go, before you bring trouble here. Go!" She made shooing motions with her hands.

"The horse's previous owner is in a dungeon in Byzas. He will not be following anyone anywhere. The Emperor of Byzas gave the horse to me." Realising she would sense the lie, he amended it to, "Well, he asked for someone to ride it. I mounted and it flew me here. Now,

I need to get it back to him. Somehow."

She softened, somehow. "You slept out here last night? You must be freezing. Come into the kitchen, where you can thaw out in front of the fire while you tell me everything." She held out her hand.

He longed to kiss it, but he doubted she wanted his lips on her gloves.

She laughed. "You and kissing."

Mind reader. Of course. She had read his thoughts that day. And seen fit to grant his wish. Kisses from an angel…

"Come to the kitchen."

Whatever Lady Penelope asked, he could not help but obey. So he did.

Nineteen

It wasn't until she had Godfrey seated beside the kitchen fire, wrapped in her cloak, that she remembered her cooking skills were non-existent, and there were no servants in the kitchen to help her.

But there was bread, and she knew where the cheeses were kept in the buttery. Oh, and she still had most of the oranges she'd picked. They would do nicely in some mulled wine — and even she could manage to make that.

That would do to break her fast, and his. It was the first day of Lent, after all.

She peeled and sliced the oranges, dropping them into the small pot she'd used for this purpose more times than she could count. "So, you're Sir Godfrey, now? How did you become a knight?"

Godfrey shrugged. "My father thought it was a suitable occupation for a younger son who was good with horses. It took a couple of years to get good enough with a sword to be made a knight, that's all." The moment he closed his mouth, he began berating himself for telling her how useless he was. He was a fool…

She handed him a slice of orange. "I wouldn't call you that. You're the only man clever enough to work out what my gift is. When I first met you, you were more boy than man, and so thin a good ocean breeze might blow you away. Two years of sword practice has put meat on your bones, and given you more confidence than you possessed back then. I didn't recognise you at first." She smiled and sank her teeth into her own slice.

He sighed. "You will think me a fool, when I tell you what I have done."

"We all do foolish things at times. It does not follow that we are all fools." She set the pot over the fire and turned to meet his gaze. "You have my deepest condolences for the loss of your sister, may God rest her soul."

Something broke in him then, releasing a torrent of images that told a far more tragic tale than the words spilling out of him.

The marauding crusader army, finding his sister, joining the crusade…and waking in Byzas. The loss of his favourite horse.

Tears coursed down her cheeks as she tasted his despair, as he suffered blow after blow. A lesser man would have given up, but not Godfrey.

She finished straining the wine and poured two cups. "So you lost one legendary flying horse, and became the unexpected owner of another."

Godfrey shook his head. "No, that thing out there belongs to the Emperor of Byzas. I have no doubt he'll want it back, though I have no idea how to manage that. Short of loading it onto a ship headed there. As for heading to the Holy Land to catch the crusaders who killed my sister…I fear I have lost any chance of that. Why the horse would take me here, of all places…"

Penelope passed him a cup of mulled wine. "Perhaps I can help you. Tell me again about the magician, and what you did to make it fly."

She sipped from her cup as she let his words wash over her, focussing instead on the images running through his mind. A magician who had touched something on the horse's neck to fly. Godfrey had pricked his finger, too, as if paying a blood price…

"Is there magic in your family? Your mother, or grandmother, perhaps?" she interrupted. It was rare for magic to manifest in men, but not unheard of. Men might carry magic in their bloodline, passing it on to their children and grandchildren, but it was girls who tended to show signs of extraordinary gifts from it.

"My mother, and maybe my sister," Godfrey admitted.

If she and Godfrey had a daughter, she would definitely be a witch. Penelope almost choked at the thought. Thank heaven she was the mind reader, and not Godfrey.

"I could take a look at your horse, and see if I can help you get it to fly again," she said.

His eyes lit up. "Would you?" Hope kindled within him. Hope that he might be able to catch the crusaders, save his sister's honour and avenge her...

He would die, Penelope knew with a certainty she could not explain. If he fought four knights again, or even one of them, he would die. There were enough fools and wicked men in the world. To lose one good man on a fool's errand...no. The world needed good men.

"But I would have to come with you," she added. The moment the words left her lips, she wanted to take them back. She could not leave Rialto. Her father, her friends, the nuns here at Saint Angelo...

His eyes widened. "War is no place for a woman! If you knew the things the infidels have done...or the crusaders..." He fell silent as he realised she'd seen it all in his thoughts. "How can you bear to see such things and not be frightened?" he whispered.

She wet her lips. "Slave ships. When northern armies take prisoners, they bring them here in chains, to be shipped to wherever slaves fetch the best price. I hear...all their thoughts. What they have already suffered. What life is like on the slave ships. What fate awaits them..." She shuddered.

"By all that's holy..." Godfrey reached out, as though he wanted to take her in his arms and comfort her, but he did not dare.

"The Emperor of Byzas took thousands of Rialto citizens prisoner, and they languish in his dungeons still. Ordinary citizens, merchants and their families, who lived in Byzas until the emperor's troops dragged them from their homes and seized everything they owned." She swallowed. "The previous Duke, Vitale, was supposed to go to war against Byzas to rescue them, but he went crusading first, and lost most of his men. Too many to take Byzas. My father is Duke now, and he promised to bring our people peace. So that our captured citizens are not sent to the slave ships next. And he hopes...hopes that if I marry one of the Emperor's sons, he will let our people go." She let out a breath she hadn't known she'd been holding. Before Godfrey could say anything more, she continued, "I will help you with your horse, if you will take me to Byzas, so I can see the truth for myself. Whether our people are still alive, and whether I can save them."

Because if she knew she could truly save them, she would no longer be a coward. She would tell her father to make the match, and marry her off to some faraway prince. Even if she couldn't save them, she would save Godfrey from dying in a crusade.

Madness had stolen her wits, she was sure of it. She'd never left Rialto. To travel to Byzas, the imperial capital, with a man she barely knew…

A man currently staring at her, with awe in his eyes. He'd thought her an angel before, but now he was certain. "I will take you anywhere you wish. I will defend you and your honour with my life. And I swear upon my sister's memory, I will see you safely home when your work in Byzas is done."

He meant every word.

Only a coward would refuse him. A coward

who wanted to go back to her weaving, and not worry about the rest of the world.

She held out her hand. "Then we have an accord, Sir Godfrey. Give me a moment to pack some provisions for the journey and then we shall depart, without anyone the wiser. We'll be back before anyone has a chance to notice my absence."

Twenty

Godfrey followed Lady Penelope out to the garden, where he'd left the enchanted horse. She didn't stop until she stood beside it.

"How do I get on it?" she asked.

He showed her the step cut in the horse's side, offering his knee to help her climb high enough to reach it.

"You look like a natural," he said when she settled onto the horse's back.

She laughed. "Don't lie, Sir Godfrey. I look like what I am – a nervous rider, her first time ever sitting upon a horse."

He didn't dare argue. Instead, he swung up behind her. Thank all that was holy for his armour, for without it, her body would be pressed against his and he could not help his thoughts from wandering to where they shouldn't...

"This is hardly the time to think about kissing, Sir Godfrey!" she said. "How two people could do such a thing while riding on horseback...it is impossible, I am sure."

He busied himself with tying her sack of provisions to the horse's otherwise useless tail.

"Ready?" she asked. "Now, if memory serves correctly, you pricked your finger on a nail on the horse's neck, pictured your heart's desire, and the horse flew you here."

Godfrey felt his face redden. He knew he did not deserve her, was not worthy to be her husband, but any man who knew her could hardly help but love Lady Penelope. Surely she knew that.

She laughed again, then stopped abruptly. "I'm not laughing at you. But if you knew...most men do not like me. They fear me, finding my eyes too knowing for their liking. If they knew I could read their every thought…they would kill me for sure. It is a rare man indeed who truly values a woman above his own desires. You underestimate your worth, Sir Godfrey."

More likely she overestimated it, out of the goodness of her heart, but he did not say it. She would be a Byzas princess, possibly one day the Empress, and he was a mere baron's son. She did him more honour than he deserved, allowing him to be her knight protector on her visit to Byzas.

She leaned over, feeling for the protruding nail. A sharp intake of breath told him she'd found it, and he watched in wonder as the horse rose smoothly from the ground. Higher and higher they went, until the whole lagoon spread out beneath them.

"I've never seen it like this before. So beautiful," she breathed. The horse stayed where it was, floating just beneath the clouds, as if she had no greater desire than to feast her eyes on the splendour of her home.

On his first flight, he'd been too afraid of falling to admire the view. Lady Penelope was indeed a wonder.

"My valiant knight protector won't let me fall," she said softly, before directing her gaze across the water. "Now, on to Byzas." At her command, the horse began to move.

Twenty-One

Sir Godfrey proved a particularly delightful travelling companion. Not only was he a solid weight at her back, sheltering her from the wind, but he was particularly knowledgeable about the places below them, for he'd travelled through many of them since leaving his home.

In one town, Pegasus had thrown a shoe, and it had taken both Godfrey and Zoticus to rouse the inebriated blacksmith, and several tries before the smith had managed to fasten the shoe on the right hoof. In a tiny hamlet, every man of fighting age had chosen to take up the cross and march with the crusaders. When he'd left another village, he'd discovered a cat had given birth to a litter of kittens in his saddlebag, and Zoticus had nearly expired with laughter as Godfrey had needed to don his gloves over his bleeding hands to evict the mother and her offspring – wrapped in his warmest woollen tunic, for the cat could not be detached from the wool without ripping it to pieces.

Waterwheels that turned mills, men who lived most of their lives on horseback, their homes little more than tents that travelled in their saddlebags, ruins of cities older than living memory...it was like listening to him telling tales of the infidels conquering the Holy City, only better, because this time his words came with rich images from Godfrey's memory.

"I talk too much, my lady. Surely you have plenty of tales to tell."

She shook her head. "I spend most of my day weaving and sewing. I could tell you a tale about the trials and tribulations of weaving my friend's bridal veil, but I fear it would put you to sleep. I'm much more interested in tales of your adventures. Please…will you tell me what happened to the cat? Did you find her a nice, warm barn somewhere, or…did they even have barns in the place where you found her? Or were you among those tent people?"

He laughed, and continued where he'd left off.

Penelope did not want the ride to end, but she knew it must. At least she had the return journey with him to look forward to – for he was determined to see her safely home.

"Where in Byzas do you wish to go first?" Godfrey asked.

Penelope shrugged. "Just set down somewhere that there will be space." If Byzas was anything like Rialto, there would be open space near the prison and the palace, and both would not be far from one another.

Godfrey chuckled. "At least I am not the only one to underestimate Byzas. Wait until you see the city." He pointed over her shoulder.

Penelope squinted. She thought she could see the ocean, white foam as waves broke on hidden rocks and shoals, and behind it.…

She gasped. Walls rose up from the sea itself, impossibly high and white, stretching for miles until they curved back around the largest city she had ever seen. Why, Rialto would fit inside those walls ten times over. Maybe more.

Penelope took a deep breath. "The prison, then. There is no point going to the palace unless I'm sure my people are still alive."

The enchanted horse responded to her wishes, landing in the yard outside the prison. People crowded around the edges of the yard, and on the walls of the prison, pointing.

Penelope had never seen so many people in one place. Not even at the trial of the pigs, when all of Rialto turned out to see justice done.

"I should stay to protect you while you do…whatever you need to," Godfrey said, reaching for his sword.

Fear rippled through the crowd…and Godfrey, too. One sword was little use against a mob of thousands.

He knew it, but his vow would not allow him to leave.

Penelope scanned their thoughts. Their fear was tempered by curiosity – the people were not a mob, and were more likely to run away from the flying horse than toward it.

To tell the Emperor that his horse had returned, she realised the same time as Godfrey did.

"Perhaps we should fly to the palace first, so I can show the Emperor I have returned unharmed with his horse," Godfrey said.

She took a deep breath. "You go to the palace, and do what you must. I will stay here with the horse and…find out what I can." When he hesitated, she added, "Should anyone approach me, I will fly away."

Godfrey eyed the prison walls. "There are archers up there."

She managed a smile. "I shall fly higher than their arrows, and return after dark, when it is safe."

Finally, he nodded. "Promise me you will stay on the horse's back. If there's anything I learned in my knight training, it's that you have the high ground on horseback – and the advantage over anyone who isn't."

She patted the worn wood. "I will be here when you return."

He dismounted, then strode across the yard until he vanished into the crowd.

Alone. Alone, amongst thousands.

Penelope drew in a deep breath, then expelled it slowly. She cast her gift wide, a net encompassing the prison. Pain and despair hit her first – from the dungeons where the guards tortured criminals for information and their own enjoyment – but she moved deeper into the building.

Despair swirled through her mind, thicker here, but the pain had dulled somewhat, to a niggling ache that would not go away.

A child's voice rose above the rest – outraged that he was required to do his schooling without his abacus.

Penelope couldn't help but smile. Definitely the child of some Rialto merchant. She had found them.

Thousands of her people, crowded into cells, filling cellars that had once held provisions. Grim, resolute, worried, fearing no help would come, and yet…still there was hope. They might be prisoners, but they had not been tortured. Families huddled together, hunger gnawing at the edge of their thoughts as they waited for their dinner. A dinner that would be paltry compared to what they'd enjoyed in their own homes, but enough to survive.

Hostages. That's what they were. Not ordinary prisoners, but ones the Emperor planned to release. At least, that's what their leaders believed.

The only way to find out would be to ask the Emperor himself.

Or read his thoughts.

One man among thousands…millions, maybe.

But she knew Godfrey's mind, and he was headed for the Emperor. He approached the palace even now, climbing the steps to the throne room. Telling his business to the herald, who nodded and sent a messenger to the Emperor himself.

The present petitioners were from one of Rialto's rival port cities. Without their hats, she couldn't be certain which one, but the smudged ash on their foreheads marked them as members of the same faith as her own, instead of the eastern one more common in Byzas.

Hatred for the petitioners burned from one of the men at the base of the dais. An old warrior, accustomed to commanding troops, but willing to wade into the fray with his sword until the blade ran red. He wanted to do that now. To slaughter the petitioners and everyone like them who did not share his eastern religion. When the Emperor succumbed to his illness and his young son took the throne, this general intended to seize power, be named regent, and order the massacre. He was practically salivating at the idea.

Shuddering, Penelope sought some thoughts that were less…horrifying. She turned to the child on the dais, who could not have been more than six years old. This was Alexios, the Emperor's eldest son, and his mind was a stormy tantrum the like of which Penelope would have expected in a toddler. He wanted to play and eat sweet things and not stand on the dais with his father. Only the fear of another blow from his father stopped him from giving voice to the screaming tantrum.

Her father planned to marry her to that spoiled child? The marriage could not be consummated for a decade, at least. Would she be able to bear children then? Not for long. And the young Emperor would need heirs…

She shook her head and plunged into the Emperor's thoughts. He, at least, was listening to the petitioners, but nothing they said would change his mind. They wanted him to give them the imprisoned Rialto merchants' property. Something he could not do, for he'd seized it to fill his empty treasury.

As he would surely seize her, and her dowry…

No wonder Father had not finished negotiating her betrothal to this prince. The Emperor would seize her dowry, leaving her barren and penniless. Probably imprison her with her people, where she would wait until the Emperor died and the bloodbath began…

Her breath caught in her throat, and she could not seem to draw any air in. Choking, she bit down hard on her lip to block all other thoughts from her head except her own.

Spots obscured her vision, as she became aware that the constriction in her throat was real, not imagined, as a man's hands tightened around her neck.

Fly…fly! She threw herself forward on the horse's neck, desperately reaching for the nail.

But blackness found her first.

Twenty-Two

"This audience is at an end. All those who desire an audience with His Imperial Majesty, assemble outside the doors at dawn on the morrow!" the herald announced.

Godfrey jerked out of his reverie, and moved to follow the crowd. The herald seized his arm. "Not you. You are commanded to stay, and show the Emperor this horse immediately."

Immediately meant something different in Byzas, Godfrey soon learned. The Emperor required refreshments and a change of clothing while his coach and a squad of guards were assembled at the palace gates. This included a horse for Godfrey to ride as he led the procession. He had to duck his head to hide his amusement at this unasked-for gift of a palace horse, too late for it to be of any use to him.

But it would get him back to Penelope sooner. He wished he hadn't left her alone, but what danger could she come to in broad daylight in a very public square? As she'd said, she had the enchanted horse – she could easily fly away from trouble. Yet he could not help worrying.

The crowd outside the prison had dispersed, probably headed home for dinner. Or perhaps they didn't trust their monarch not to send them to the dungeons for getting in his way. Neither would have surprised Godfrey, not after what Penelope had told him. To imprison thousands of your own people simply because they came from a particular city. One of your loyal subject cities, no less. It beggared belief.

A shout came from ahead, and Godfrey urged his horse to move faster.

He reached the yard outside the prison…the empty yard. No horse, no Penelope. "Oh God." Godfrey slid from his horse and dropped to his knees to pray she was safe.

"Up there! Shoot him, shoot him!"

The cry came from behind him, and it took Godfrey a moment to realise what the guards were pointing at. The enchanted horse floated high above, with a cloaked figure atop it, and a bundle draped across the horse's neck. Something dropped from the bundle, plummeting to the ground.

Godfrey scrambled to his feet and ran to reach it first. It was Lady Penelope's boot, still warm.

Someone had stolen her and the horse.

"Don't shoot!" Godfrey bellowed, waving his arms. "He's got Lady Penelope of Rialto!"

"Who?" the Emperor demanded, sticking his head out of the carriage window like some peculiar kind of sideways turtle.

"That's the magician! He used some sort of magic to escape from his cell!" one of the guards at the prison gate shouted.

The Emperor's eyes narrowed. "And his

countrywoman helped him escape. I knew Rialtines weren't to be trusted, and this proves it."

"She did…she wouldn't…" Godfrey began. But he didn't know, not truly. Perhaps she had planned this all along, duping him into helping her…

No. If she'd gone willingly, she would have sat astride the horse, as she had on the way here. Not thrown across the horse like baggage. Somehow, the magician had overpowered her so he could steal the horse from her. That's what had happened.

"The man who brings me that magician's head may have my daughter's hand in marriage. And if you bring me the woman as well, I will give you anything you ask." The Emperor met Godfrey's gaze for a moment, before disappearing back inside his carriage. The carriage and escorts circled around the yard, then headed back the way they'd come.

Leaving Godfrey alone in the yard with the Emperor's horse beside him and the enchanted horse shrinking in the distance as it headed north. Back toward Rialto.

Godfrey tucked the boot into his belt and mounted up. Where Penelope led, he would follow. The magician would lose his head, and all would be right in the world again.

Twenty-Three

Pain woke Penelope. Her midsection ached like her courses had come early, and her head pounded worse than any hangover she'd ever endured. One of her feet was blissfully numb, but she did not know why.

She forced her eyes open, but the darkness remained. It took her a moment to realise it was night time – how long had she been unconscious? And where was she?

She felt around carefully with her hands, and found nothing but smooth, hard wood. Somehow, she'd fallen asleep on the horse.

No, not fallen asleep. Someone had choked the air from her lungs, rendering her unconscious, and left her…outside the prison, in an unfamiliar city?

No, she could feel a breeze upon her face. A breeze not unlike the cold caress of the clouds as she'd flown with Godfrey…

Penelope swallowed. She was flying on the enchanted horse, thrown across it like some chattel. And the man riding it had done this. A man who was definitely not Godfrey. Why take her at all? Why not leave her behind?

She concentrated on his thoughts, holding tight to the horse as she tried to divine his intentions. His attention was fixed on the land below. No, the lagoon below, for in the pre-dawn light she could discern the islands of Rialto. Home.

His thoughts clashed with hers, a wave of anger and betrayal at a city he wished would vanish beneath the waves. Because he could never go back there, after being exiled. A rich city, a religious city, where he'd been ready to settle down happily until they threw him out. But even then, his luck had held. He'd found the ancient, enchanted horse, in the ruins of a forgotten city, and flown back, offering it to the Duke for a pardon and a marriage alliance. But the damned Duke had dismissed him and his horse…

Penelope was startled to see her own father's face in the man's thoughts. This man had wanted her to be his wife? Who was he? Not some foreign prince, if he'd made his home in Rialto.

Home. So close…

She fumbled about on the horse's neck, searching for the nail that would draw her blood and give her control of the beast. Her greatest desire right now was to go home, and take this man to her father. He'd nearly strangled her, then kidnapped her – more than enough reason to deserve death, the punishment that would be meted out to a returned exile.

An exile she had no doubt he deserved, whatever he'd done.

The man's voice interrupted her thoughts. "Oh, you're awake, are you? No, don't do that…"

Without warning, he slammed her head against the horse, hard, and darkness took her again.

Twenty-Four

Rialto never changed, Godfrey thought, as a gondolier – perhaps the same one as before – poled him to the Ducal Palace. Where Penelope's father now lived.

Godfrey gave his name to a manservant, and settled down to wait. The ruler of Rialto was a busy man. Much like the Emperor of Byzas, he would have far more important matters to deal with than an uninvited visit from a foreign knight.

"Sir Godfrey! What a pleasure!"

Godfrey's head jerked up. Rialto might not

have changed, but Sebastiano had aged considerably in the years since he'd last seen him. But the Duke's smile was as genuine as ever.

"My l — I mean, Monsignor…I've come about Lady Penelope." Godfrey swallowed. How did you tell a man you'd run away with his daughter, only to have her stolen from you, and spirited away? Duke Sebastiano might be older than his father, but Godfrey had no doubt the man could best him with a sword. Penelope's honour would demand no less than his death.

Sebastiano smiled indulgently. "The sweetest daughter any man could be blessed with. She has joined the convent at Saint Angelo of Concordia, and I cannot imagine a more fitting place for such an angel. I visit her there as often as time permits."

Godfrey had to pause to process the Duke's words. He had found her at a convent, but she hadn't mentioned being a nun. No, she'd definitely talked about marriage. Unless she'd lied…

And rescued the magician, his traitorous

mind added.

Godfrey shook his head. He wouldn't believe that of her. Couldn't.

"When did you last visit her?" Godfrey managed to say.

Sebastiano looked thoughtful. "Why, it must be a week ago, perhaps longer. She left the convent to attend a friend's wedding, on the last day before Lent. My duties as Duke keep me busy here."

He didn't know. Didn't know that he'd taken her.

Or maybe he did, and the Duke was lying, to keep Godfrey from seeing her again.

"Could you…send word to her that I am here? I wish to know that she is well," Godfrey said, hating the awkwardness in his voice, but what else was he to say? He could hardly tell him the truth. He wouldn't leave here alive.

"I had planned on sending her a gift this very day. A chest of fine silk skeins, for her weaving. The finest weavers and dressmakers in the city have begged to be allowed to clothe her, but she will have none of them. She weaves and makes her own clothes. She even made her friend's wedding dress for the wedding last week, though neither the bride or groom was a pauper. Why, my daughter is the envy of every dressmaker in the city, for none can make gowns like she does." Sebastiano beckoned to a servant. "I shall send a note with it now, to tell her of your visit, and your kind enquiry after her health."

The note was written and despatched, before the Duke invited Godfrey to join him for dinner, later in the day.

Godfrey could not refuse, so with a promise to return later in the day, he departed.

He considered hiring a boat to take him to the convent, so he could see for himself if she was there, but he had no guarantees that she would see him. Even if she did, could he bear to look her in the eye, knowing she'd betrayed him? If she had…

Even her father likened her to an angel. Surely they couldn't both be mistaken.

He wasn't sure what he wanted to hear — that she'd betrayed him, but was now safe at home, or that the magician had kidnapped her, and she was now in the devil only knew what kind of danger.

A branch scraped his shoulder, and for a moment, he thought it was a grasping hand. No, just bare sticks, the first signs of spring blossom starting to show on the branches above. He didn't know what sort of tree it was, or what fruit it might bear in the heat of summer. Penelope would – that day they'd kissed, she'd had leaves in her hair, and he'd plucked one to keep. He still had it at home somewhere, a reminder of that perfect moment.

He prowled through the trees, until he found a small church dedicated to Saint Mark. Patron saint of this city. The city Penelope said her marriage would help to save. No, not just the city, but its people – the prisoners the Emperor kept in his dungeons. Was even that a lie?

God, he did not know any more. What was true and what was right and what he should do. First Melisende, then the unknown girl in Byzas, and now Penelope...what kind of knight was he, if he could not protect those who could not protect themselves? Never mind Melisende's killers – he was the one who didn't deserve absolution from joining the crusade. That's why he'd lost the army, and the enchanted horse, and now Penelope, too.

Maybe the magician was right, and he was cursed.

Godfrey fell to his knees and prayed. Not for himself – he didn't deserve the saint's attention – but for Penelope, who had seemed so earnestly to want to save her city. To keep her safe. Because if he could save only one woman in his life, it would be her.

Hours later, or so it seemed, a hand touched his shoulder.

"Sir Godfrey, the Duke is about to sit down to dinner."

Godfrey climbed laboriously to his feet – he must have been kneeling for longer than he'd realised – and followed the servant to the Ducal Palace.

The dining room seemed empty without Penelope, though the Duke and plenty of servants were present. Godfrey wasn't sure why he'd hoped…

"Sir Godfrey, please, sit." The Duke

gestured to the seat across from him. "I must beg you to forgive my servants for interrupting you while you were at prayer, but I had an inkling you might need to hear this news sooner rather than later."

Godfrey sat, and a cup of wine was thrust into his hand. He wanted to deny his desire to hear whatever news the Duke might have, but he couldn't. Not if it pertained to Penelope.

Let her be safe at the convent. Safe and well, no matter what else she had done. Safe and well, and he would forgive her anything, Godfrey prayed silently.

"The servant I sent to the convent has returned," the Duke began. "It seems my daughter is not at home. No one has seen her since the start of Lent."

Godfrey's heart sank down into his boots. He could not bear to meet her father's eyes, knowing it was his fault this had happened.

Wordlessly, he pulled out her boot and set it on the table. He wished it still retained her warmth, but it had gone cold before he'd even left Byzas.

"What has happened to her?" the Duke

demanded.

Did the Duke have dungeons, where he tortured people? Godfrey wasn't sure he cared. Not knowing what had happened to Penelope, while knowing it was his fault, was agonising enough.

Godfrey wet his lips, hoping the Duke was not a mind reader like his daughter. "She was taken from the convent by a man on an enchanted, flying horse. He took her to Byzas, where she was seen briefly. She dropped her boot as he flew off with her, headed north. I had hoped he came here, as the magician claimed to have come from Rialto."

The colour drained from Sebastiano's face. "A man with a magical flying horse? Oh, no. Poor Penelope."

"What? Who is Lord Valerio?" Godfrey demanded.

"I know of no man of that name. But I do know a man who claimed to have an enchanted, flying horse. Leonardo Gabrieli, a pretend priest who seduced nuns and other virtuous women, then accused them of being possessed by the devil so that he might end the affair, before returning to hear their confession and accept money for many masses to be said for their souls. Money he kept for himself, for he was not a priest at all. He was exiled when it all came out, for the courts deemed death too good for him.

"One of my trading ships marooned him on an uninhabited island to the south, and that was all I heard of him, until a few months ago. He sent me a letter, thanking me for choosing that island, for there, he'd unearthed a trove of riches, including a priceless magical artefact – an enchanted, flying horse. He offered it to me in exchange for recalling him from exile, and giving him my daughter to be his wife. Naturally, I refused. No father who loved his daughter would willingly give her to the very devil himself."

Godfrey squeezed his eyes shut. What had he done?

He rose. "I swear to you, I will find her, and bring her home to you. The Emperor himself has already called for the magician's head. I pray I will be the first to find him, so I can deliver that to you, as well."

The Duke rose, too. "Bring her home safely, and I will give you anything you ask."

Rescuing Penelope from the devil's clutches would be miracle enough for Godfrey, but he did not say that to the Duke. "I would walk through the gates of hell itself, if that's what it takes to find her," Godfrey said instead. Seeing as he was probably headed to hell anyway now...

Sebastiano slumped into his seat. "Pray it does not come to that, Sir Godfrey."

Twenty-Five

"At this rate, we might have to ride to the Holy Land itself before we find a suitable quarry," Prince Magnus complained. "The crusaders have wiped out anything larger than a mouse."

The other courtiers laughed, though it sounded forced, but Count Vesone did not. Prince Magnus might be a spoiled child who knew between little and nothing about hunting, but he was not wrong about this. Count Vesone's lands would take decades to recover from the ravenous host that had devoured everything in their path on their way to save the Holy Land. He only hoped the price he and others paid would be worth it. That Emperor Frederick and his army would return victorious. Anything else was…unconscionable. Just the thought of Prince Magnus on the throne…

"I'm hungry!"

Count Vesone gestured for his servants to start laying out the midday meal. The teenage prince was annoying most of the time, but when he was hungry, he was unbearable. Better men had met with hunting accidents in the past…

Besides, there was little point to hunting in an empty forest.

A forest that had fallen silent.

For all Magnus's complaints, there had been birds, and rustlings from small creatures. But now there were none.

A woman's scream rent the air, a shrill blast from her lungs followed by an equally piercing plea for, "Help!"

Vesone leaped easily into the saddle, while the other courtiers stood frozen, as though they'd never heard a woman scream before. If

Magnus were truly to become Emperor one day, he should have been the one to issue the command, but he was as slack-jawed as the rest.

"Come, we must help her!" Vesone called as he rode in the direction he thought the voice had come from.

As if to spur him on, she screamed again.

Not waiting for the others to catch up, he urged his horse to speed up.

He found them in a clearing – the very spot he'd hoped to reach for their midday meal. The man had the girl backed up against a tree, one hand around her neck, a knife in the other.

"Step away from the girl," Vesone commanded, laying his hand on his sword.

The man glanced behind him, but his grip only tightened on the girl. "This is no business of yours, sir. I'm merely teaching my wife a lesson in obedience, something she has been slow to learn, and we are here so that we will not disturb the neighbours with the noise." The knife came to the neckline of her gown, poised between her breasts. "Isn't that right, wife?"

"I am no man's wife, least of all this piece of exiled scum!" the girl said, baring her teeth. "I am Lady Penelope of Rialto, and he kidnapped me, knocked me unconscious and dragged me here –" His grip on her throat tightened, choking off her words and her air.

Vesone expected her to claw at her throat, to get him to release her, as the bloodied scratches on his hand said she already had, but the girl surprised him. She grabbed for the knife, and succeeded in making him lower the blade, but not before it had sliced down the front of her gown.

"I said step away from the girl." Vesone dismounted and drew his sword. He didn't know who to believe. If the man was right, it would take him very little time to discover the truth from whatever nearby village they'd come from, and he could do what he wished with his unwilling wife.

If he was lying and the girl was telling the truth, justice must be served.

The girl kicked him in the shins, forcing him to loosen his grip on her as he stumbled back.

"I demand justice!" she said. "This man is

Leonardo Gabrieli, exiled from Rialto by my father, the Duke of Rialto, for crimes so numerous and vile, death was deemed too good for him. For daring to enter the Rialto lagoon, his punishment is instant death, and I demand immediate justice from the lord of these lands!"

A whistle sounded from behind Vesone. Magnus and the others had finally joined him, and the young prince's eyes were fixed on Lady Penelope.

And no wonder, for Gabrieli's blade had slashed her gown open to the waist, baring her breasts and the red line of trickling blood between them. Perfect breasts heaving, as her eyes fixed firmly on Vesone. Demanding his assistance, as any lady of her breeding would.

"Lying whore!" Gabrieli hissed, raising his fist to strike her.

Vesone didn't hesitate. He thrust his sword between the two, so Gabrieli's blow landed on the blade, cleaving his arm open to the bone.

Gabrieli howled, turning his knife on Vesone instead.

An arrow sprouted from Gabrieli's throat.

Gurgling, the man clawed at it, before falling to his knees. His eyes burned at Vesone, blaming him for his impending death, before the light in them died and he toppled over at Lady Penelope's feet.

She looked down with distaste, and only then did she notice her own nakedness. She tried to pull her torn gown up to cover her breasts, no longer the lady in charge. Now she looked like a frightened girl as her eyes met Vesone's again.

"I call it a successful hunt after all!" Magnus cried, holding his bow high over his head in triumph. "I claim the kill, and the prize."

Lady Penelope gave a delicate shudder, shaking her head almost imperceptibly. Magnus meant to claim her as his prize, Vesone realised in disgust.

Vesone unfastened his cloak and wrapped it around Lady Penelope. "Come, my lady. I am Count Vesone, and these are my lands. Now that justice is done, please accept my hospitality, and the services of my healer."

She hesitated a moment, then gave him her hand, and allowed him to help her onto his horse. She sat at the back of the saddle, not touching the stirrups or the reins. As though she had no idea how to ride a horse.

Or had Gabrieli injured her worse than he'd thought? By all that was holy…how did he ask a lady to speak of unspeakable things?

She managed a timid smile. "Thank you for such timely action, Count Vesone. If you had not intervened, I fear that brute would have had his way with me. He was a magician, possessed of diabolical powers that could bring things to life. He rode on that wooden horse, using his magic to make it move." She pointed at a life-sized carving of a horse. Though it stood in the middle of the clearing, he hadn't noticed it until now.

"Then it shouldn't be left here, for anyone to find. Not if it is tainted by dark magic," Vesone said, beckoning for a servant to come forward. He left orders for the carving to be brought into his castle, where it was to be locked in a dungeon. Just in case.

He eyed Lady Penelope, averting his gaze from the pouting prince who couldn't keep his eyes off the injured girl. She would need an escort, for if she lost too much blood, she might fall from the saddle.

As if reading his thoughts, the girl swayed, appearing pained.

"Continue the hunt. I will take Lady Penelope home to find a healer," Vesone said. He mounted the horse before her. "Hold on to me, my lady."

Twenty-Six

Count Vesone's castle was like something out of a story. A square, stone building, several storeys high, with a tower keep stuck to one side, soaring above it.

The tower occupied his thoughts, too — for that's where he planned to put her. For her safety, he told himself repeatedly, as he planned to place guards on the level below hers, and perhaps the stairs as well.

The Count was true to his word, shouting for a healer as he helped her down from his horse. "Can you walk?" he asked anxiously, already stretching his arms out to carry her.

Her wounds stung, especially where her clothes clung to them, but the cuts were shallow enough. She could climb the spiral stair to the top of the tower. Better than being carried up them, for all the Count's gallantry.

"I can," she said softly, pressing a hand to her chest as if it pained her. He fancied himself her honourable protector, and it cost her nothing to feign weakness. She was aching, tired, in need of a bath and a good night's sleep, and she had no idea how to get home without his help. He would help, too – he was no twisty Byzas courtier, to simper and smile while debating how best to kill her. Nor was he a gold-driven Rialto merchant lord, trying to work out the best way to profit from the situation.

He led the way up the tower stairs, pausing occasionally to make sure she followed. "This was the original keep, built by my ancestors in the time of Charles the Great. My great-grandfather had the second castle built, and he pledged to build a cloister on his land, too. Construction took longer than he expected, and for a time, the nuns stayed here, in the tower, until the cloister was finished."

From one convent to another, Penelope thought. She was destined to die an old maid, just like Marco the fake fortune teller said.

Vesone caught her frown. "It fell into disuse until my father died, and my widowed mother decided to take the tower room for her own. She has been gone these ten years, but the servants keep it as she left it, a chamber befitting their dowager countess, for she was well loved. There will be clothes and all the things a lady needs there. You may take whatever you wish. If anything is not to your liking, I will make arrangements to improve it for you, for you cannot travel until your wounds have healed." And it would take time to assemble a suitably large guard to protect her on her journey home to Rialto, if indeed she was who she said, he added in his head.

Penelope nodded. Every step higher became more and more of an effort. If she'd known there would be so many steps, maybe she would have allowed the Count to carry her. Now, she just hoped the climb would soon end so that she might rest.

When she reached the top, the brightness in the room dazzled her, forcing her to stop. She blinked, bringing into focus the windows letting in so much light. They were made of horn, much like the ones she'd had at home, but cut into a delicate diamond pattern. "It's beautiful," she breathed.

Vesone bowed. "I'm sure you wish to rest. When the healer arrives, I'll see that she is sent to you immediately."

He departed before she could respond, but Penelope was too busy examining her new quarters to notice.

The dowager countess had been a weaver, too, judging by the loom placed in the brightest part of the room. Chests around the walls held linens, silks, and wool in myriad colours – all waiting to be woven into something new.

A small chest at the end of the narrow bed held what remained of the woman's clothes, all in mourning black and grey. Penelope grimaced. She had no intention of mourning the magician, but she'd prefer even grey garments to ones stained with blood.

There was water in the jug, so she decided to wash while she waited for the healer.

Off came the Count's cloak, but her own clothes were another matter. Her torn gown and chemise had stuck to her wounds as the blood clotted, and she hissed with pain as she pulled them free. Her cuts started bleeding anew as her shredded bodice settled over her skirt like some horrible parody of Marzia's wedding lace. The bloodstained wash water trickling down to turn it red did not help matters.

"Oh, don't do that, dear. Let me clean those cuts properly," a new voice said.

Only now aware that she was bare to the waist, Penelope lifted her arms to cover her breasts from the newcomer's sight.

The middle-aged woman made a clucking sound in her throat. "Healers see plenty of skin, dear. Let's get you out of that ruined gown and onto the bed so I can tend you."

Penelope took a moment to skim through the woman's thoughts to determine that she truly was a healer before she stretched out on the bed. A blissful sigh escaped her at the much-needed softness.

The healer set to work, unpacking her satchel on the table.

"You're a lucky one. If this cut had gone any lower, and just a little deeper, it would have opened your belly, and you would not have lived this long," the healer said as she worked. Some of her ministrations stung, but Penelope gritted her teeth and wished the ordeal to be over.

"But without you, the future won't work, so I suppose even fate has her favourites. Can't kill the loom you're weaving on," the healer continued.

"What?" Penelope blurted out. Her head felt clear, but the healer's words made her brain feel fuzzy all over again.

The healer shot her a sharp glance. "Empires rise and fall, and only a select few will ever know why. You have the power to make peace between emperors and kings, Lady of Rialto. But power calls to power, so you will give the world five powerful queens, though you will never take the throne for your own."

"How…" Penelope began, reaching for the woman's thoughts. A jumble of images waited for her. Her own face, but older, never alone. A dark-haired woman, her skin tinted faintly blue, as if underwater. A girl surrounded by fire, battling a dragon. A blonde teenager holding a thorny rose, heedless of the blood trickling down her hands. A fair girl with red-rimmed eyes, eyes that reflected fire both without and within. A redhead across the water, an army breaking like waves at her feet. And herself as she was now, hair flying in the wind, as she flew the enchanted horse high above three armies, marching on Rialto. "You're a seer!"

The healer inclined her head. "Yes, and I've been seeing visions of you for as long as I can remember. You're younger than I thought you'd be. I'd wager you haven't even bedded that handsome husband of yours yet." She winked.

"I will marry after all?" Hope rose in Penelope's breast. "Are you sure?"

The healer chuckled. "Nothing is certain in a seer's visions – for your gift has shown them to you as surely as mine has given them to me. But when the fate of empires rests on you choosing wisely, I can say with certainty that one of the queens will be the daughter of your union with the man you love." She blinked. "Or will love, if you don't yet."

"Who?"

"I'm only a seer. I see the future, not the secrets of your heart. That's your gift, dear." The healer patted her shoulder. "If you put on a clean shift, I'll take these rags away for you, for I've done all I can for you now. Rest, recover, and when you're ready, the opportunity to leave will come. Your fate lies far from here, over the water." And with that, the healer left.

"Wait...I don't even know your name!" Penelope called after the woman.

"You may call me Mistress Dalia, though I doubt we'll meet again. Have courage, Lady Penelope, and keep busy."

Twenty-Seven

"I don't care what promises you made! You are nothing without my father, and in his absence, I am the highest authority here. I will have her!"

At first, Penelope though the petulant cry belonged to a woman, but a quick peep into the spoiled brat's thoughts revealed it to be the boy she'd seen yesterday. The one who'd been so overwhelmed with desire at the sight of her bare breasts, desire that had reached fever pitch when blood welled, and he'd killed the magician to get to her. Without the Count's quick thinking to cover her and spirit her away, heaven only knew what the boy would do.

"She is Lady Penelope of Rialto. The Duke of Rialto's daughter. If you have her against his will, you will start a war. An attack on her person is an attack on Rialto itself, and not something those merchants will take lightly."

"But I want her!" the boy whined. "She's only a duke's daughter. No one would know..."

"Rialto has no king. No emperor. They are ruled by a duke – a duke who happens to be her father. As far as Rialto and the rest of the world is concerned, that girl is a princess, at the very least. The man who kidnapped her...there will be pursuit. Even now, Rialto's armies will be searching for her. If they find out she was here and came to harm, they will have no mercy. I will send a letter to her father tonight, telling him she has been found, safe and well, asking how we might best return her home. For if we do not and she is found here...all our lives will be forfeit."

"Then fetch a priest – I'll marry her, and bed her right away! What God has joined, no man may sunder."

Ugh. Penelope shuddered at the image in the boy's head – of her own naked body, bloodied as if from a battle, thrown down on the ground as he had his way with her.

"If her father finds out she has been forced into a marriage not of his making, he'll sunder plenty. Starting with separating your head from your body. Please reconsider, Your Highness. Your father would never forgive me for starting a war or being responsible for the death of his favourite son."

The prince's pride nearly exploded at the Count's glib lie. "Then send the letter to her father. Tell him the Emperor's favourite son wishes to marry her."

Relief flooded through Vesone. "I will, Your Highness."

"Good. Now, take me to her. I want to tell her myself." Another lie. What the prince wanted was to see her naked again, and he hoped to catch her undressed, at the mercy of a healer.

"But she has been through a terrible ordeal, Your Highness. I fear if we disturb her before she is properly recovered, it may cause irreparable harm…"

"Don't be silly, Vesone! She's going to marry me. That's the best news she could ever hear. I have no doubt it will put her in the best spirits!"

Penelope wanted to laugh at the prospect of sharing a bed with that bloodthirsty toad. Better than the vipers of Byzas, but not by much.

"I'll even honour her with a kiss!"

Could she endure kissing a toad without throwing up? She suspected she was about to find out, as she heard the sound of feet on the spiral stair. She glanced around, wishing she had something she might use as a weapon to defend herself. But she was no warrior – she was a weaver. Which, in this room, might be enough…

Penelope placed herself behind the loom. A distaff sat propped against the wall, within easy reach, and the unusually large shuttle would work in a pinch. Why, this one might do double duty as a rolling pin in the kitchens. A formidable weapon indeed, if she had the strength to wield it.

And if she didn't?

She sank onto the stool, her knees no longer willing to hold her. So much for the healer wishing her courage, for hers had fled through some tiny gap in the horn windows.

The boy appeared in the doorway, closely followed by Count Vesone.

"Lady Penelope of Rialto, may I present Prince Magnus, son of His Imperial Majesty?" Vesone said.

Bloodlust burned in the prince's eyes, until his gaze fell upon her modest grey gown. Then fury replaced it. "What is she doing here?" He waved his hand up and down. "And why is she wearing that?"

Vesone bowed as low as he could. "My deepest apologies for the interruption, Lady Penelope. His Highness commanded me to take him to you, and as I have always been His Imperial Majesty's loyal servant..." If he'd refused, the prince would have demanded his head. The prince did not understand that, as the Duke of Rialto's daughter, she was the prince's equal, if not his better, for Emperor

Frederick was not fool enough to make an enemy of Rialto.

Only a queen could cow the prince. So a queen she must be.

Penelope inclined her head, not bothering to rise. "Thank you, Count Vesone. He looks like a fine boy. I'm sure Emperor Frederick is very proud." She forced herself to lower her gaze to the empty loom. She picked up the shuttle and pretended to go back to her weaving.

This only angered the prince even more.

"Stop that!" the prince insisted, striding forward. He reached for the spindle.

Without thinking, she rapped the spindle across his fingers. "Don't touch my work! You'll ruin it."

His eyes widened in fear as he stuck his stinging fingers in his mouth. Then he looked at the loom. "There's nothing there!"

Of course, he was right. She hadn't even strung the warp threads on the loom, let alone begun weaving properly. A ridiculous tale of her mother's came to mind, and she said, "Just because you cannot see it, does not mean it's not there. Rialto weavers are among the finest in the world, and Rialto lace so fine that it is almost invisible to the common eye."

If he'd heard the same tale, he'd challenge the lie at once, but it seemed the prince had not. He was too busy pouting at being struck, and plotting how he would have his revenge when they were married. "Keep weaving, then. When you are well, I want to see you wearing a gown made of this on our wedding day." The prince turned and trotted down the steps. All the way down, wondering whether the fabric on the loom was real or if she'd gone mad. Only a madwoman would dare strike a prince...who knew what else she might do? The wedding would have to wait until the Count's healer had cured her madness, for he would not tolerate being struck again.

Vesone stared mournfully at her, as if he wanted to say something, but could not form the words. He thought her mad, too.

If madness might buy her time, then mad she would be.

"How do you like my Rialto lace, Count Vesone?" Penelope asked, gesturing at her empty loom. "Is the colour too bright, or should I add more of that gold silk to it? I'm sure I saw some…" She moved to the nearest chest and began rifling through it, looking for the imaginary gold thread.

With her back turned, she should not have seen him poke a finger, then his whole hand, through where the cloth should be. But of course, she saw all that in the Count's mind, and more.

"Get well, Lady Penelope," he muttered, as he hurried down after the prince.

To write a letter telling her father she'd lost her wits, and to send someone to collect her soon.

Ooh, there was gold thread here – skeins of the stuff. While she waited, she might weave something real, as well. Heaven forbid that she should wear a widow's mourning clothes when her father's men showed up. No, she wanted to wear the brightest colours imaginable on that joyful day.

Twenty-Eight

Godfrey had lost count of the days he'd been riding north, not to mention the tiny inns where he'd spent the night. They all seemed the same, with watery ale, thin stew with more vegetables than meat, and beds with mattresses worn so thin it was a wonder he slept at all.

"I have a tale that can top them all," a newcomer boasted, slapping both hands on the bar. "Keep my cup filled with ale all night, and I will tell you everything!"

Judging by the excitement this caused in the small country inn, Godfrey suspected news had been hard to come by of late. A pile of coins formed on the bar – enough to buy the man a meal as well as enough ale to see him sleep for days, no matter what mattress he lay upon.

The innkeeper dipped a mug into the ale barrel and set it before the storyteller.

The newcomer took a deep breath. "Now, every man here has heard of the Holy Crusade our Imperial Majesty, Emperor Frederick is on, right? Him and two of his sons, while the oldest stayed at home to rule in his father's place. The younger boys all got fostered out across the kingdom. One of the princes, he got sent to a castle not far from here. It belongs to the Count of Vesone."

The storyteller paused, to drink the health of the Count he served, before continuing: "One day, the Count takes the young prince hunting. They go deep into the woods, far from any road or town, where no one goes. And they hear a woman scream. A woman where there should be no one.

"So they ride deeper into the forest to find her. When they do, they are just in time to save her from a terrible rogue who has stolen her away, and means to steal her virtue, too."

He drained his ale, then waited for a refill.

"The girl is fair fainting from fear, but the Count manages to revive her, and asks for her tale. How she came to that place, and who she and her attacker were."

The storyteller slapped his hands on the bar. "Who do you think she was?"

Various men shouted names, from their favourite whore right up to queens from legend. He shook his head, laughing at them all.

"She said the man was a magician, who flew her from her home on a magic horse. Then she said she was the Duke of Rialto's daughter, the highest lady in that land. The Count, being the wise man that he is, believed her at once, for such was obvious from her noble bearing, and offered her the hospitality of his home."

Again, the assembled men toasted the Count's health. Godfrey's grip tightened on his cup as he willed the storyteller to continue.

"Ah, but the prince...do not forget the young prince! Not yet a man, but near enough to know a beautiful woman when he sees one. And she was – the most beautiful girl there ever was seen, dazzling the poor prince, who fell instantly in love with the girl."

There was some laughter at this. They had never seen her, Godfrey had to remind himself. She would enchant most men, if it truly was Penelope.

"Sadly, she fainted again before she could fall in love with him, and they carried her to the Count's castle. A healer came to see to the girl, and said she would live. The prince was delighted, and sat by her bedside, day and night, waiting for his beloved to wake up."

Anger burned in Godfrey's gut. The boy might be a prince, but how dare he remain in Penelope's bedchamber while she slept? She would be horrified if she knew.

"It was some time before she awoke, this beautiful lady, and she beheld her prince, her rescuer. The prince fell to his knees, overcome with her beauty once more, as he beseeched her to marry him."

Another pause as the storyteller drained his ale. One man congratulated him on a good story, hoping the prince would be happy. The storyteller nearly choked at this, and the taproom fell silent.

"Happy? The prince? Oh, the story is not over yet. For the damsel in distress, the sweet maiden who had swooned in his arms, was a completely new creature upon waking. As though possessed of the devil himself, she attacked the prince so violently that he feared for his life, and fled her chamber. The Count was forced to lock the girl in the top room of the tower, so that she could not hurt anyone in her madness."

No. Penelope would not threaten a man's life. She might throw an orange at him, but want to kill him? Godfrey could not believe it of her. This girl must be someone else, pretending to be Penelope.

The storyteller brandished a scroll case. "The Count has sent me with a letter to the Duke of Rialto, asking him to send someone to fetch his mad daughter. But the prince, oh the poor prince! The prince wants the Duke's permission to marry the girl, mad or no, and offers a reward to the man who can cure the girl's madness. To the man who can lift the curse from her – for it is the magician's curse, I have no doubt, likely whispered with his last breath as he lay dying – the prince will give a bag of gold and his sister's hand in marriage."

Cheers erupted, as the patrons drank to the health of the prince, the storyteller and the promised princess.

Godfrey had to wait until the crowd around the storyteller had dispersed before he dared approach the man.

When the storyteller turned to head up the stairs to the room he'd undoubtedly secured for the night, Godfrey made his move.

"Is that sailor's tale you told true, man?" he asked.

The storyteller turned around, narrowing his eyes. He'd had several mugs of ale, but not enough to be drunk, Godfrey judged. "I swear it on my life," the storyteller said.

Imprisoning Penelope… "Did the Count truly lock her in a prison?"

"In a tower," the storyteller corrected. "The dowager countess's bower, in fact. Not a prison at all, but where the Count's late mother did her weaving and sewing. Far superior to any other sleeping chamber in the castle proper. The prince still means to marry her, when someone lifts the madness. In the meantime, she can be heard, working on the dowager countess's loom. It is the only thing that calms her."

Penelope had mentioned her affinity for weaving and sewing. Perhaps…

Godfrey held up a silver coin – more money than the inn patrons had laid on the bar, much of which had ended in the storyteller's pockets. "Tell me her name."

The storyteller eyed the coin. "I cannot quite recall. It was a long name, a name from legend. Panacea. No, that's not right. Persephone? No…ah, I remember now. It was Penelope."

His throat suddenly too dry to speak, Godfrey handed over the coin and dismissed the man.

He'd found her.

When the sun's first rays touched the earth the next day, Godfrey was already well on his way north to Vesone. To save Penelope from princes, counts and whatever curse the magician had cast.

Twenty-Nine

Word had spread of her supposed madness. Servants tiptoed in and out of her chamber, fearful of her notice. Penelope longed to say something that would dispel the miasma of fear that surrounded her, but she didn't dare. Fear was the only thing that kept the prince away, though more than once she'd heard him climb the stairs to peep through the keyhole to her chamber. Hoping to catch her in a state of undress, she knew.

The next time a servant came, she'd complained about the door's eyes staring at her and demanded a screen to hide her from view. The poor maid had nearly flown down the steps, but the screen had arrived soon after, to the prince's endless muttered frustration.

The loom was a good one, and she wove until she ran out of gold silk. It was not enough to make a whole gown, so she searched through the chests for more.

The dowager countess had left enough supplies to make a lifetime of clothing, but she hadn't liked gold thread much. Or maybe she had, and she'd used it all. She'd also liked weaving green wool, with swathes of cloth filling three chests.

Perhaps Penelope should make a gown from the already woven wool, to wear while she wove something brighter than the dark green the countess had favoured. She started to spread the cloth out, measuring it with her eyes. There might be enough for one gown, and half enough again for a cloak to match, but it would be best to do the cloak entirely in dark green. Then she might melt into the forest, and no one would see her.

Which she would not do until she had no

other option.

Penelope dug through the chest, lifting aside a bundle of black wool to find more green. Yet this cloth was not the same as the rest. Soft, like felt, yet gleaming like silk. If she'd been asked, she would have described it as short fur, if any creature alive had moss green fur. Yet the stuff had clearly been woven on a loom of some sort.

She laid it out atop the wool. Enough for a gown, and she could trim it with the gold silk. She would keep the scraps of the green stuff, though, in the hope that she might manage to replicate such strange cloth. The green wool would become a cloak, then, for this stuff shimmered too much when it caught the light.

She would cut and sew the gown and the cloak in secret, hiding them when she heard the thoughts of anyone climbing the stairs. When they reached her room, they would find her seated at the loom, weaving the invisible Rialto lace that made them all think she was mad.

What she would give to see real Rialto lace again. To feel the stuff under her fingers as she'd fashioned it into a wedding dress for Marzia…Penelope wiped away a tear that had appeared, inexplicably, on her cheek. She would go home. It might take all her courage, and fortitude, and endurance, and many other virtues she wasn't sure she possessed, but Count Vesone had written to her father, and her father would send someone to escort her home, if he could not come himself.

When she saw him again, she would wear a green cloak, over a green and gold gown made of the mysterious cloth. Ready to give the world…was it five queens? And bring two emperors to heel. Her. One woman, a weaver, who would be happy to spend the rest of her life simply creating clothing.

Perhaps that was it – she would clothe five queens in such magnificence that men swooned and lost their hearts to them. Even emperors were men, too, with all the urges of the flesh.

But these mysterious queens must wait, for her own gown came first. Yes, the gown, then the cloak.

Decision made, she set to work.

Thirty

Vesone's castle was much like his father's, Godfrey mused. Sitting on a hill at a distance from the town…but Vesone's tower was part of the castle, not on a neighbouring, higher hill, like his father's. A tower where the Count kept Penelope, if his messenger was to be believed. He squinted at the tower windows, hoping for a glimpse of her, but they were all shuttered. Never mind. If his plan worked, he would see her soon enough.

He'd sold his horse at the last town, covering his armour with a coarse robe like those worn by the Benedictine monks. Nobody at this town paid him any attention as he headed past the inn, toward the monastery on the edge of town.

"I'm Brother Iudas, a mendicant friar from Saint Angelo of Concordia," he told the first monk he met. "My abbott told me to travel here, for he was told in a dream that my healing skills were sorely needed."

The monk frowned. "We have a good healer here already, who can cure many an illness. You may stay for a night, if the Abbott agrees, but your own superior must be mistaken."

Godfrey lowered his voice. "My abbott is never mistaken, and I know he is not now. On the road, I heard tell of a terrible affliction that has befallen someone at the castle. I am no ordinary healer. God has blessed me with the miracle of being able to cure madness."

He prayed he would be forgiven for the lie. Though it would not be entirely a lie if he could restore Penelope to her sane self. If such a thing was even necessary...

The monk nodded. "I will take you to the Abbott. Father Danilo will know what to do."

Father Danilo and the Abbott were one and the same, so Godfrey only had to repeat his tale once, adding details about Saint Angelo until the man seemed satisfied.

The priest was only too willing to take him up to the castle, for he confided, "Count Vesone is very worried for the young woman. He feels responsible for not protecting her properly, and is willing to do anything within his power to be able to return her to her father, healed."

No more than Godfrey himself. He hoped the priest's assessment of the Count was indeed accurate.

The priest took him to the Great Hall, where a servant promised to tell the Count of his arrival, before begging the priest to pay a visit to the servant's mother, who lay dying in her bed.

Godfrey waved the priest away. "Go, see to the poor woman's soul. I can meet with the Count alone."

The servant thanked them both profusely, beckoning Godfrey to follow him up to his master's solar, because, "I can see you are a holy man of God, and I will vouch for your goodness myself."

Feeling more uncomfortable by the minute, Godfrey followed the man upstairs.

"My lord, this is Friar Iudas, who Father Danilo assures me is an expert in matters of madness and possession."

"Send him in."

The servant waved Godfrey into the room, then shut the door behind him.

The silver-haired man dressed in plain wool might have been the castle steward, not its master, but the vair collar on his cloak gave away his high station. "Do you believe I gave the devil leave to take lodging in my home, Friar?"

Godfrey considered for a moment, then replied, "I believe the devil is a tricky beast, one which may hide its true nature in order to steal souls it does not deserve. I have seen madness from other sources, too — sometimes a curse can make men behave contrary to their natures. I would need to see the patient for myself before I could give you an honest answer to your question, my lord."

The Count nodded. "Very well. I'll take you to her."

Part of Godfrey wanted to tell the Count to wait, but the rest of him was simply too eager to see Penelope again. If it was Penelope…

He fairly flew up the stairs to reach her, stopping only when they reached the closed door at the top.

Count Vesone rapped on it three times. "Lady Penelope, may I enter?"

That voice. "Yes, of course, Count Vesone."

Godfrey nearly fell to his knees to thank heaven and all their saints for their help in finding her. Not least of all Saint Iudas, patron saint of hopeless causes. But he remembered himself, and hoped the Count didn't notice.

"Are you coming, Friar?" Vesone asked in a low voice.

Godfrey swallowed. "I will stay here, and observe unseen. If the devil sees me, he will surely recognise me, and perhaps set the poor girl upon me, where she might be hurt."

The Count nodded. "Very well." He strode into the room, and asked Penelope about her weaving.

Godfrey edged into the room, placing himself behind a large screen that presumably blocked draughts from the door, and looked his fill.

She was dressed in dove grey, which made her brilliant hair stand out all the more. She kept her eyes down on her loom as she told Vesone about her work. A soft smile played about her lips, just as it had when she'd listened to Godfrey's stories.

Perfect Penelope, showing no signs of madness or ill health. His prayers were answered.

After a while, the Count finished his conversation, and made to leave. Godfrey hustled out of the way before she saw him, for if she recognised him and called him by name, the Count would know he had been tricked.

When the door closed behind him, the Count shook his head. "Madness has taken hold of her wits completely, I am afraid. She speaks of cloth that does not exist, yet to listen to her, one would believe she could see it! Is it the devil, or a curse, Friar? And, more importantly, can you cure it?"

Cloth that did not exist? There was a tale his uncle had once told him about such cloth. Cloth sold by a greedy Rialto merchant to a particularly prideful emperor. A pretence, so that those who knew the merchant might see the emperor as he truly was.

Penelope could be feigning madness, but why would she do so? He needed to speak to her alone.

Godfrey deepened his frown. "I am not certain. I must know more. Tell me, how often does she attend church?"

"Never. Why, she has not even been to confession, though it is Lent."

Godfrey nodded thoughtfully. "See that she attends confession tomorrow. With Father Danilo's help, I will prepare a trap for the devil, if indeed there is a devil, and force the beast out of her."

It was the Count's turn to frown. "And if you cannot?"

"Pray that I can, my lord."

Thirty-One

"The Count says you must dress for church, milady, and prepare for confession," the maid told her when she brought Penelope's breakfast.

Oh, how many sins she would have to confess. Or was that conceal?

Feigning madness, striking a prince, wishing the prince would choke on his dinner and die, her satisfaction at the magician's death…the list was long, and not one she cared to confess to a priest who might tell all of it to Vesone.

She chose to wear the green gown, trimmed

with gold, as she'd finished sewing it only yesterday. No one but she and the maid would see it, though, for she left the tower shrouded in one of the dowager's dark mourning cloaks.

Half a dozen of Vesone's men surrounded her to shepherd her into town. Not to the church, but the monastery. None of the men seemed to know why, for their minds were filled with more questions than her own. They left her at the door, where she was escorted by a single monk to the refectory.

She almost told him she had no need for an escort, for this building was the twin of Saint Angelo. She'd heard a tale that Saint Angelo had originally been built for monks, who had given it to their sisters when a more suitable site, closer to the city, had been gifted to the community. Now she saw the truth of it.

Yet this refectory had one item that the one at Saint Angelo did not – an ornately carved confessional, where laypeople might confess their sins to the priests in the community, and receive absolution at the hands of these holy men.

The monk opened the door for her, and

then closed it when she was inside. Trapped inside a tiny box, barely big enough for one person...oh, there was a good reason why she only endured this once a year.

The priest was no less fearful as he entered his own wooden cell.

"Forgive me, Father, for I have sinned. It has been close to a year since my last confession," she began, wondering what to say next.

"Tell me your sins, child," the priest prompted.

The priest's fear increased, and Penelope took a moment to work out why.

She almost laughed when she realised he was frightened of her. Well, not her exactly, but the demon he believed possessed her, driving her to madness. And he had some sort of plan to rid her of the creature, a plan that involved both the Count and a newcomer to the community, a holy man whose business was disposing of demons.

"Child?" the priest repeated.

Penelope shook her head. If the priest meant to hand her over for the ministrations of some quack, she fully intended to make him question his own conscience, too. "My greatest sin is overwhelming fear, Father. Fear that the plan in place for me will be more than I can bear. Fear that that I may never go home again. Fear that I will be held prisoner here…I fear every day, Father, that those who profess to help me do not have my best interests at heart, and that I am wrong to have faith in them and their plans for me." Even Dalia the seer expected too much of her. She was one woman – how could she be the one to make kingdoms rise and fall? Elevate not one, but five queens?

"You must have faith, child, in God's plan, and no other…" He thought she referred to the demon and its plans, not his own. Or hers.

"I fear I have lost my faith, Father. And I know not where to find it."

He seemed satisfied with this response. "Then that will be your penance. You will pray until your faith once again finds you."

No, that didn't make sense. "But, Father – "

The door to her cell opened, and a strong hand grasped hers.

"My brother will take you to my private chapel, where you will remain in prayer until your faith is renewed," the priest said.

"No – "

Do not resist, my lady, and your prayers will be answered, along with my own.

The words hung in the air, unspoken, yet clear in her mind.

She stared at the monk who held her hand. With his face hidden beneath his cowl, she could see nothing but the strong fingers that enveloped hers.

Come with me, my lady.

She wished she had the power to push her own thoughts into the minds of others, instead of the other way around. She would tell his man to stay out of her head and shove his prayers up his own arse. She bit down hard to stop the words from leaving her lips.

The monk bowed his head in obedience – almost as if he'd heard her! – and moved away, tugging her after him.

Try as she might, she could not break free from his grip. She would be forced to follow him.

He pulled her into a short passage, then kicked the door shut behind them. Only then did he tug off his cloak and drop it on the floor.

Godfrey stood before her, grinning.

Her mouth dropped open, and no words came out.

Please do not say you have lost faith in me, my lady. I have searched so long to find you.

She threw her arms around his neck and kissed him. Not the tentative sort of kiss they'd shared in her father's house, all those years ago, but something crafted out of all-consuming passion and fire that burned all her doubts away.

"Get me out of here, Godfrey," she begged, breathless.

He pressed a finger to his lips, and pulled her though the passage and down into the chapel proper. Candles sat on every surface, with filled candelabras forming a rough circle around the centre of the floor. Someone had scrawled strange symbols on the flagstones, in what looked like a mix of chalk and blood.

"Godfrey, what – "

He shook his head, his finger not leaving his lips.

The priest is listening. He has never performed an exorcism before, and hopes to learn how by spying upon us. And the Count sent his own spy, a young squire who hid behind the confessional, so that he might hear what you said. I know he has not gone far…

The clear images in his mind illustrated the tale. Godfrey had mistaken Prince Magnus for a squire – what a blow to the boy's pride, if he but knew.

I have a plan, but in order for it to work, we will need the enchanted horse. Do you know where it is?

Penelope shook her head. She hadn't seen it since the day the magician died. When blood had bubbled up from his mouth, as he'd gasped for his last breath…

Even closing her eyes could not shut the image out. Her lips sought Godfrey's, so that she might lose herself in the warmth of his embrace. The warmth of his thoughts, as he wrapped his arms around her, before he pushed her up against a low wall of some sort, his body pressed against hers, the heat of them together more than she could bear, and yet…and yet, she wanted to lean back, to open herself to him, in every way possible…and he…he wanted…

To make love to her on the altar.

By all that was holy, they could not do something so wicked!

I did not know you could do that.

She looked up at him, a question in her eyes.

I heard you, as clearly as if you'd spoken the words aloud. Just like when you said I should shove my prayers…

Her cheeks flamed.

Please forgive me. You may not have guessed, but I have attempted few quests, and I have not yet succeeded in completing any of them. I promised your father and you that I would bring you safely home, and I mean to do so. But if you do not know where the horse is…

Penelope took a deep breath, then lifted her lips to his ear. "The Count has it. He had his servants bring it to the castle, but he locked it away, for he fears it."

She felt the sigh gust out of him, as relief relaxed his shoulders. Then all she could feel was his lips on hers as he whirled her around, incoherent with joy.

Her heart swelled within her chest, sharing his joy…or expressing her own? Who could say? Reading the secrets of her heart was her gift… Dalia's words washed over her, revealing the truth she had not known until now.

It wasn't joy, or not just joy. Her heart swelled with love for Godfrey, the knight who would save her, whatever the cost.

She bit her lip, tasting blood, then fixed her gaze on Godfrey's face. *Do whatever you must to free me of this place. I trust you.*

He bowed deeply. *I am honoured by your trust, my lady.*

Thirty-Two

His lips burned from her kisses. Though he knew he was not worthy of a single one, he had not been able to resist her. Nor had he wanted to.

But when she'd said she trusted him, he knew her honour depended on him finding the fortitude to play the part he'd created for himself.

So he did not allow his lips to linger on hers for another moment, no matter how he longed for her touch. He donned his hooded monk robe once more, willing her to trust him still, as he scooped her up in his arms.

She stared at him, shocked.

I am going to tell them I attempted an exorcism, but the demon fought so hard, I feared it might kill you. You swooned, and I will wait until you wake before I try again. Tomorrow.

She nodded in understanding, then lay back in his arms in a most artful swoon.

He would have given everything he owned to see her lying in his arms like this. Now, he didn't want to let go.

If you let go, I shall fall, so I implore you, do NOT let go. He could even hear her tart tone, as though she'd spoken the words aloud.

Never, my lady.

If only she could be his lady…

He half expected the guards waiting outside the monastery gates to take Penelope from him, but they kept a healthy distance from her as they surrounded him, and escorted them back to the castle. He carried her up the tower stairs and laid her on her bed, cloak, boots and all, wishing he dared to steal one more kiss, but he could feel the maid hovering behind him, waiting to tend to her mistress. He had to force himself to leave her chamber and close the door.

The Count pounced on him. "Is she healed?"

Lady Penelope was as perfect as the day he first met her, he wanted to say but did not dare, or all this would be for naught.

Godfrey sighed deeply and hung his head. "The devil within her is uncommonly strong. We fought long and hard, until her delicate body could take no more, and she fell into a deep swoon. But before she did, the devil said he had been driven from his true vessel by a magician, and had been forced to possess the girl against his will. His true vessel was much larger, a sort of sinister, dark horse, or so he said." He tried to appear puzzled. "Have you ever seen such a thing? Or has the girl?"

Vesone slumped. "Yes, there was a large, wooden horse where we found her. I feared it was something dangerous, so I locked it in the dungeons."

Godfrey forced himself to look surprised. "So there is such a thing? Demons are so skilled at lying, I suspected there would not be, but if there is…we must take the chance. Both the girl and the demon will be weak for some days yet, so we should act quickly. Let her sleep now, but when she wakes, have her and the horse brought to the town square, along with all the incense you can find. Then, I shall force the demon from her and into the horse, before I burn it to ash."

Vesone bowed deeply. "If you succeed in curing her, you will have my gratitude, and that of His Highness as well. As men of your order do not marry, perhaps a different reward will be offered…"

Godfrey shook his head. "Freeing the maiden of this diabolical taint will be reward enough." Lies, every word. He hoped the Count did not know it.

"You are truly a saint," the Count said.

Oh, if only he knew.

Thirty-Three

"My lady, you must wake. If you cannot walk, the master's men will carry you. Maybe even the prince himself."

Little toad. The distasteful thought of the prince made Penelope open her eyes. She'd rather throw herself from the top window of the tower than let the prince get his hands on her.

Especially after Godfrey's kisses yesterday, before he'd carried her in his arms…

She wished she truly was the swooning type, so that she might sleep and dream of it all over again. But it was tomorrow, the morrow Godfrey had promised her, when he would take her home.

She wore the green gown again, and the cloak she'd made, with a pair of boots the dowager no longer needed. Just like yesterday, guards surrounded her for the short walk to town, but instead of the monastery, they took her to the town square, where a number of bonfires had been prepared. They circled around the familiar figure of the enchanted horse.

A number of townspeople stood in the square, asking whispered questions of one another. None seemed to know why there were bonfires or a horse, until someone spotted her.

"They're going to burn the devil out of that girl."

She wasn't sure whether the man had spoken aloud or merely thought the words, but the statement spread like wildfire until everyone seemed to be staring at her in a mix of fear, excitement and dread. None of them had seen an exorcism before, or a devil, but they were determined to witness this.

As long as they didn't truly mean to burn her.

Godfrey wouldn't do that.

But if this wasn't his doing…

Two guards pushed her into the circle and backed away from the wood piles.

She whirled, just in time to see the first bonfire kindle into flame. All around her, torches were thrust into the oil soaked branches, until they belched out smoke, rising up into the sky.

She wanted to back away, but the fire blazed on all sides. There was nowhere to run.

Her back hit something hard. The enchanted horse. She climbed onto its back, reaching for the nail that would draw her blood.

Please, do not leave without me, my lady. Godfrey slid onto the horse's back behind her, wrapping both arms about her waist.

The smoke was so thick, she could not see the crowd, though she could hear their shouts. She and Godfrey rose up, level with the rooftops, then higher still, following the smoke that hid them until they reached the clouds.

Safe. Free.

Thank all that was holy, for her courage was spent.

Penelope burst into tears, letting her fear drain out of her with the endless salt water. Somehow, she'd turned to bury her face in Godfrey's tunic, and his arms around her were exactly the kind of comfort she needed.

"Lady Penelope, with your permission, I would like to take you somewhere you will be safe, where you can rest, a stop along the way to taking you home to Rialto."

It took her a moment to realise he'd spoken aloud. She swallowed, her throat dry and scratchy from the smoke. "Yes," she managed to say.

She felt Godfrey reach forward over the horse's neck, heard his gasp as the nail drew blood. Then the horse turned beneath them, heading to the destination of his desire.

As long as it had a bed and water to wash with, she would be happy, was her last coherent thought as she drowsed in his arms.

Thirty-Four

Lady Penelope was still asleep when the wooden horse landed in the courtyard outside Godfrey's father's castle. The place had not changed a bit – not that he'd expected it to.

No servant came to see to his horse, but it wasn't as though this one needed feeding, grooming or even rest. Penelope probably did, though, so he took her up the servants' stair to Melisende's chamber. He did not dare undress her, but he took the liberty of removing her boots, and unfastening her cloak, before laying it atop her for a coverlet.

He left her there, where no one would disturb her, and went to wash and change into fresh clothes. Questioning the first servant he found, Godfrey discovered his father was at dinner in the Great Hall, and he hastened to join him.

His father's booming laughter rang out. Godfrey tensed. His brothers must be home, then. They would not be happy to see him, for surely Father would have told them about his part in Melisende's death. Poor Melisende – he had failed her in life, and now in death, too, for he would never redeem her honour now. It was a miracle Penelope trusted him, given what a failure he'd been.

Now he had to admit his failure to his father.

Godfrey threw open the doors of the Great Hall, and marched in.

"Godfrey! Is that truly you? We thought you were dead!"

Godfrey bowed to his father. "No, by some miracle, I still live and breathe, Father."

"It must be a miracle, for I just finished telling the Baron of Mareschal how you died of your wounds, after you slew Sir Enguerrand and his companions."

Godfrey blinked. At his father's right hand sat Zoticus. Who…had just said Enguerrand and the Unholy Trinity were dead? Along with he himself…

The slightest nod from Zoticus confirmed his suspicions. All four were slain by Zoticus's hand. Which meant…Melisende's honour was restored.

"So, by what miracle are you here? When I saw you fall that final time, I could have sworn you were dead, or I would not have told your father so," Zoticus said.

It took him a moment to put Zoticus's words together in his head and make sure his story matched.

Godfrey managed a pained smile. "I thought so, too, my friend, but it seems the world is not done with me yet. I woke up on a healer's cot on a ship, wishing I was dead, but most assuredly alive. When the ship landed in Rialto, I was well enough to pay my respects to the Duke, who sent me on a quest to recover his daughter." Godfrey accepted a cup of wine.

"The lady is tired from her ordeal, so she is resting upstairs right now. We will continue our journey in the morning. And what of you, my friend? I thought you were intent on freeing the Holy Land."

Zoticus shrugged. "It seems the Holy Land will be harder to free than we hoped it would be. A Seljuk army, numbering in the millions, swept down on us from out of nowhere, and slaughtered many of us where we stood. If it were not for your horse with her winged feet, I might not have made it through the battle, let alone back here to bring the news to your father of your successful quest to redeem your sister's honour."

It took Godfrey a long moment to understand what the man had said. Luckily, he did not have to swallow his surprise, for there was more than enough news to astound anyone. "The crusade is over? And you brought Pegasus home?"

Zoticus nodded.

"Thank you." The words came out flat as Godfrey sat down, overwhelmed. "I am in your debt."

Zoticus waved the debt away. "Nonsense. We are friends. Your horse saved my life. I brought her home. Debt repaid."

Godfrey made polite conversation for a few more minutes before he found his eyelids sagging, threatening to put him to sleep. He excused himself, and headed up to his own bedchamber.

They would have a long way to go in the morning, but for now, both he and Penelope could sleep safely.

And Melisende's soul might know repose, too.

Thirty-Five

Penelope woke in a room with corners. Definitely not her tower room.

"Are you awake, Your Highness?"

She didn't recognise the curtseying maid, either.

"Where am I?" Penelope asked.

"Mistress Melisende's room, at the Baron of Maraschal's castle. Sir Godfrey ordered me to attend you. I wasn't sure if you wanted to dress or break your fast first. I was only in training to be Mistress Melisende's maid. I never thought I might have the honour of serving a princess." She curtseyed so low, she could have sat cross-legged on the floor.

"I'm not a princess. I'm Lady Penelope of Rialto."

The maid did not rise. "Sir Godfrey said the titles were different where you come from. That they do not call you a princess, yet princes beg for the honour of your hand. Forgive me if I offend you, Your Highness."

It wasn't the maid's fault Godfrey had told her such things. "Where is Sir Godfrey now?"

"With the horses, as always. I can send for him, if that is your wish?"

Penelope shook her head. "No. Help me dress, then take me to him."

The maid agonised over the gowns that had once belonged to Mistress Melisende, none of which she thought was good enough for a princess, until Penelope pointed at one in pale blue wool and insisted upon it. She almost regretted her choice when the maid laced it up over her chemise, for it was obvious that Melisende had been much narrower in the chest than Penelope. As it was, the lacing pushed her breasts up and out, like the bawdiest tavern whore. Only by fastening her chemise close about her throat could Penelope manage any kind of modesty.

The maid slid silk hose up her legs while Penelope braided her own hair. She felt the maid's disappointment at not being able to try out what she imagined were court fashions, which was quickly eclipsed with horror as Penelope donned the dowager's boots she'd arrived in, but the girl did not say anything aloud.

Penelope hoped the girl might one day meet a real princess, who would undoubtedly fulfil all her dreams of grandeur. Penelope herself would never be royalty – had the seer not said so? The thought was more freeing than she'd thought it would be.

The maid led the way outside the castle walls, where fields held…what was the name of a group of horses? Was it a herd? She wasn't sure, but there sure were a lot of them. Prancing, dancing, and galloping about, their hooves making the most thunderous sounds as they hit the turf. So…wild.

She backed away from the energetic beasts,

only to feel something warm and solid stop her retreat.

Something blew a gust of wind down her shift from high above, and she shrieked.

"Easy, Pegasus. This is Lady Penelope, and I'm sure she doesn't appreciate you blowing your breakfast down the front of her gown."

There was straw caught in her lacings. Now she not only felt like a tavern whore, but one who'd taken a tumble in the hay. And here was Godfrey, holding the bridle of the most enormous white horse, beaming at her as though he had no idea what she was thinking.

"My sister would be green with envy if she ever saw how well that gown fits you. You look breathtaking, as always, my lady." Godfrey bowed.

From another man, it might have been empty flattery. From him, it was the honest truth.

"Would you like to join me for a ride?" He gestured at the field of frolicking horses. "Pegasus here is the fastest, and my favourite, but you may choose any of them you wish. That bay over there will be sent to Emperor

Frederick, once the beast is gelded and trained, and the king in Kasmirus has laid claim to the next colt Pegasus produces. We don't sell breeding stock, only geldings, but the offers we've had for even a single Maraschal mare…it's more money than I've ever seen, that's for sure. But Father will not budge. With the exception of Pegasus, none of the mares leave Maraschal. And no one rides them but our family and those who work for us."

Hysterical laughter bubbled out of her. "Are you offering me a job, riding these capricious beasts I cannot even imagine how to control? I'd sooner go back to my tower than climb on the back of a beast with a mind of its own, and hooves that could crush my head!" She turned and hurried back to the safety of the castle.

"Penelope. Penelope, wait!"

If she turned around, she'd see those huge horses again. And the incredulous look on Godfrey's face. She did not want to hear his thoughts at that moment, his contempt at her fear of horses.

"Lady Penelope, have you never ridden a horse before? Not once?"

She stopped, not sure how to admit her shame.

"Of course, there are no roads in Rialto, and horses cannot walk on water. But I never imagined…" Godfrey paused. "Lady Penelope, would you do me the honour of allowing me to take you for your first horse ride? I promise to keep you safe. If any horse here should even think of harming you, I will see the beast butchered for the table before day's end."

She'd left whatever courage she possessed in that smoky town square yesterday. No. She shied away from his outstretched hand.

"Not even if we ride double, as we did on the enchanted horse? I would never let you fall, Penelope."

She swallowed. She knew every word was the truth, but…

"Emperors and kings would envy you, for this is an offer I have never made to anyone else. One ride, on the finest horse in the world. First around the field, and then, if you like, a bit longer. I would not offer if I didn't think you would enjoy it."

Oh, how could she refuse? He had done so

much for her, and all he wanted was to share a simple pleasure that was the greatest gift he thought he could offer.

He grinned, as if she'd spoken into his mind. Perhaps she had. Godfrey swung up into the horse's saddle, and held out his arms to help her up.

By all that was holy…

She landed in his lap. He wasn't wearing armour today, but he didn't feel any less hard behind her or beneath her.

"Shouldn't I be sitting behind you? I thought that's what ladies do in stories about knights."

Godfrey burst out laughing. "If we're ever riding into a battle and I'm wearing armour, then you can sit behind me while I shield you. But if you're going to learn to ride today, you'll need to be the one in front, holding the reins. You're the knight in training, which I guess makes me…the lady."

She had to laugh at that. Just the thought of Godfrey in a gown…

Godfrey reached around her, his arms warm at her waist. "Now, hold the reins like this, and nudge the horse with your knees, like this."

The horse set off at a slow walk. Godfrey showed her how to persuade the horse to turn when they reached a corner of the field, but she suspected this one would have turned anyway. They made it back to their starting point without any mishaps, and she dared to relax.

"More?" Godfrey asked.

She swallowed and nodded.

"I'll take you on Pegasus's favourite trail," Godfrey said, steering the horse away from the castle. "No need to tell her what to do here, she knows the way. All you'll have to do is hang on."

He leaned forward, pushing her down against the horse's neck. For a moment, she resisted.

"Be easy, and lean into it," he murmured into her ear. "Read the horse's mind, if you will not read mine, and do what I do."

She relented, letting her body move with his, and the horse. It was almost soothing, the slow lumbering gait…

"Go," Godfrey breathed.

The horse burst into flight, in a flurry of thundering hooves and rushing wind and…and…Godfrey's laughter in her ear as he urged the horse on. Not that the beast needed the encouragement. For Penelope could feel the horse's mind, too, a rush of exhilaration at running so fast. It was almost as though man and mare shared the same thought…

A low stone wall approached at alarming speed. She felt muscles bunch, tighten, and all three of them went soaring over the top of it, with barely a pause in the mare's stride. She heard a whooping sound, and it took a moment to realise it came from her own mouth.

She could feel Godfrey laughing behind her, and she laughed right along with him. The wooden horse had never felt anywhere near as fast or as exciting as this.

When the horse felt she'd galloped enough, she started to slow down. By the time they reached the river, Penelope thought she could have matched pace with her, walking beside her. But she had no desire to move from her current position, wedged firmly between the man she loved and his horse.

Until the horse stopped beside the river, and dropped her head for a drink.

Only Godfrey's grip around her middle kept her from sliding into the river, face first. He swung her off the horse, then dismounted behind her.

There was a question in his eyes, but his thoughts were so tangled, she wasn't sure which one he wanted answered.

So, she said, "Thank you. For the ride, for your patience, and for not giving up on me."

"I could not let a woman of your courage, and your determination, remain in fear of one of the gentlest, noblest creatures that ever lived," Godfrey said. "You've ridden a flying horse, and it didn't daunt you at all. I clung to its back for a good half hour before I dared to open my eyes, and then I was so afraid of falling off I didn't dare move until it landed in your orchard. I've ridden real horses for as long as I can remember, and I was terrified of a wooden one." He ducked his head, not meeting her eyes.

"I know. While you were telling me about it

in the kitchen, I was watching the memories that flashed through your mind."

"Then you know I'm not much of a knight. Horses I can handle, but quests and swords and all the other things are not my strength."

She smiled. "You saved me just fine. That makes you the finest knight I've ever known."

Godfrey didn't agree, but he had the good manners not to say it aloud. "But a poor host, taking you riding before breakfast. I should take you and Pegasus home, so you can enjoy proper Maraschal hospitality and Pegasus can get a rub down."

"Will Pegasus fly again?" she asked.

Godfrey eyed the horse. "Not willingly. She prefers open fields to the road, and the road is the fastest way back."

"Then will you be the knight this time, so I can experience being a lady?"

Godfrey laughed. "Even if you donned my armour, brandished a sword, and rode Pegasus into battle, you would still be very much a lady."

A lady who had to go home to Rialto, and do what was right. Make peace, marry, and make her father happy. Never mind whatever the future held for empires and queens. Oh, how she wished she could stay here with him. And his horse.

Perhaps if she thought hard enough, she might find a way to do all of those things.

Thirty-Six

Penelope settled deeper into Godfrey's arms as they flew, letting out a sigh of contentment. She couldn't explain why she felt so comfortable with a man she barely knew, yet she did. His embrace felt like the most natural place to be, and her thoughts strayed back to their kiss in the chapel. The sheer thrill, bubbling through her blood, as their lips touched, before the heat between them had burned deeper. Into a desire to do the unforgivable, and use the altar for a communion of body and soul that had nothing to do with the church or anyone else but the two of them. The reverence in his every touch had only made desire burn hotter, and now they were so close again, the fire had begun to smoulder within.

Of all the men in the world, Godfrey was the only one she wanted. And she had begun to believe she might be able to have him.

Penelope laughed softly. "I had begun to believe that all men below a certain age thought only with what lies between their legs, but – "

"Forgive me, Lady Penelope," Godfrey interrupted, and the delicious memory evaporated as though it had never been.

Suddenly bereft, it took her a moment to realise that the memory she'd seen was as much his as hers – they'd both been thinking about the same thing. So was the urge to lie down on the altar his idea or hers?

He continued, "I'd forgotten how you can read my thoughts, and being so close to you, I allowed my thoughts to wander into a place where they did not belong."

His thoughts fixed on an icy stream, and the

memory of jumping into the water. So cold even she gasped, pressing back against him and the reassuring warmth that the immersion was no more than a memory.

"Your thoughts mirrored my own, and you're wrong. You're not like the other men I've known. Most of them think of mastering me, possessing me, with a violence like that suffered by your sister. They do not see a face, merely a body. They mean to leave me broken, beaten, conquered, my defences battered by what they believe is a mighty battering ram but is in fact little more than a piece of gristle." She shook her head to clear the images of Magnus, Marco, and even the magician's lustful thoughts. "But your thoughts are of me, of us, of the joy in coming together, touching, wanting..." The icy clouds they flew through were not enough to cool her flaming cheeks. "I think we should find a town with an inn."

Even as she voiced her wish, she felt the horse tilt beneath them, descending. Their descent pushed Godfrey even closer to her, and she could feel him hardening at the close contact. She wasn't sure which of them blushed more.

"Please forgive me," he breathed in her ear.

The steep walls of a hilltop town loomed out of the dark, and they skimmed over the top of them, landing in a churchyard. She helped Godfrey push the horse between some bushes before taking his hand. "Now to find that inn," she said.

He pulled his hand out of her grasp. "Lady Penelope, we cannot. You are the daughter of a duke, a duchess of Rialto. Emperors and princes are willing to go to war for you, offering a world of wealth for the right to marry you. You are destined to be an empress, a queen. I am merely a knight, and a younger son at that. All your other suitors can offer you crowns, whereas all I can give you is a chamber to share with me in my father's castle, and perhaps a horse to ride. I may dream of becoming your lover, but your place is far loftier than my lowly bed. I lost my honour a long time ago, but I am honourable enough not to steal yours."

If she'd offered herself to Magnus, he would have stripped her naked by now. The magician would have done unspeakable things to her already. Yet Godfrey, sweet, honourable knight that he was, begged her to think of her own honour.

"I'm no duchess. Rank in Rialto is not like other places. My father's position is his alone, which he occupies only after the other nobles in Rialto voted to place him there. I'm as noble as you – Lady Penelope, the same rank as any knight. And so I shall remain. I will not marry the child prince of Byzas, to live in a pit of vipers, waiting for one to strike me down. I will not share a bed with that rabid cur Prince Magnus, a violent man-child who believes it is his right to have his way with women when they are unwilling." She took a deep breath. "If you truly wish to save me from a loveless marriage that will kill me as surely as any sword, then you must claim me for yourself. All honour demands is that you do so before a witness, a man of God, and that I am willing to do the same."

She felt hope rise in his breast, stealing his breath as, for a moment, he considered being granted his wish. A wish he did not believe he deserved.

Before Godfrey could protest, she marched up to the church's side door and rapped smartly on the timber. She could sense the sleepy priest inside, surprised by her knock, but coming to answer it anyway.

She threw back the hood of her cloak, smoothing her hair and straightening her clothes. The priest would not see much in the darkness, so she would need to convey everything with her voice alone.

The door swung open, and the priest lifted a lantern so that he could squint at them. "Yes?"

Penelope lifted her chin. "Good evening, Father. We wish to be married. Immediately."

The priest opened his mouth to protest.

She reached for the pouch of coins at Godfrey's belt and pulled out a handful. "We will pay you well for your trouble."

The door opened wider. "Come in."

The priest led them to the altar, and Godfrey grasped her shoulder. "Are you sure about this?" he hissed.

She merely gave voice to the thoughts running through his head, for they were no different to her own. "Marriage is for life. What God has united, no man can break apart. Be he emperor or prince or duke. You can refuse to take the oath, but I know my heart, and this is the future I choose. Marry me, Godfrey, and I will be your wife. Yours to protect…and to love."

"Are you ready to say your vows?" the priest asked.

Penelope nodded. After a moment, so did Godfrey.

"Then kneel," the priest commanded.

The priest asked for her vow. She knew her eyes were supposed to be fixed on the cross behind the altar, but she could not help looking at Godfrey.

"I vow to love and honour you, all the days of my life," she said, squeezing their joined hands. Oh, how she wished he could read her thoughts. Then he'd know she longed for this as much as he did. It might be madness, but it was the kind of madness she wanted her life long.

He wet his lips, lifting his eyes to meet her gaze. "I vow to love, honour and protect you, all the days of my life," he said.

The priest said a few more words, before pronouncing them married. United.

She wasn't sure which was more powerful – Godfrey's exultation, or her own. Did it matter?

She reached out with her mind for the inn, and found it beside the closed city gates. They were as surprised as the priest to see them, but the innkeeper was happy to accept gold in exchange for a meal and his best room.

He sent servants up with warm water to wash with, and a meal neither of them were hungry for yet. They only wanted each other.

Godfrey shooed the servants out and bolted the door.

Their eyes met and Penelope couldn't suppress her grin. "Kiss me. Please."

It was but a moment and she was in his arms again, her lips meeting his as naturally as they had in the chapel. Only this time, they would not be parted again.

Thirty-Seven

Penelope could have kissed Godfrey forever, but even newlyweds had to pause for breath. And Godfrey had more in mind than kissing, which set her cheeks aflame all over again.

"My lady, let me wash away all the memories of your ordeal." He gestured for her to sit down.

Obediently, she did.

Godfrey stood behind her, then set his hands on her shoulders and leaned forward. "I will spend the rest of my life trying to earn the precious gift you have given me," he whispered, sliding his fingers down so they rested over her collarbone.

He meant herself, Penelope realised, finding it hard to read his thoughts amid the cloud of her own desire. She wanted him to move his hands lower, to cup her breasts, to…

He unfastened her cloak, then moved away from her to hang it up. She barely had a moment to register his absence before he knelt at her feet. Off came her boots, until he cupped her stockinged foot in his hands. The silk had felt substantial enough while they were flying, but now it might as well be as ephemeral as mist, melting away in the heat of his touch as his fingers slid up her leg. Her garter halted him, but only for a moment before he ventured higher still, laying a hand on her bare thigh.

A question burned in his eyes and she had to concentrate to see the thought forming in his mind. If her stockings only went up to her knees, and he had his hands beneath all her skirts, he had only to lift them higher and she would be bare to the waist and ready for him…

She trembled at the thought, but she swallowed and nodded. Never had she been so nervous, and at the same time so eager. If he were to lift her skirts and move between her thighs, she would willingly rise to meet him. Maybe even leap into his lap.

Godfrey smiled as though he could read her thoughts now, then lowered his hand to untie her garter. He slid her stocking off slowly, stroking the silk down her skin until she shivered again, before he did the same with her other stocking. Now she knew why women covered their ankles in public. To feel the breeze caress her skin like her husband was now would drive her to distraction. Was driving her to distraction.

He lifted the hem of her skirts, bundling them into her lap to bare her legs.

Yes. Oh, yes. Please.

Godfrey laughed softly, then reached for the jug of water and a cloth. "Time to wash away the travel dust and the memories," he said, a moment before the warm, damp cloth touched her thigh. With deft strokes, he washed her leg from hip to heel, drawing ever closer to her most secret places, without actually touching her there. One leg, then the other, leaving her skin tingling and the rest of her aching for its turn.

He set the water on the table and clambered to his feet, then held out his hands. "Rise, my lady."

Her skirts tumbled down about her ankles, covering her again, yet she'd never felt so naked. The ghostly echo of his caresses even as his hands held hers, combined with the hunger in his eyes as he looked at her, saw her…it stole her breath away.

She threw her arms around his neck and kissed him. His hand cupped the back of her neck as he deepened the kiss. A thousand butterflies burst into flight in her breast, as he unfastened her shift and bared her neck and shoulders. But for the lacing of her gown, he would have exposed her breasts as well. Her fingers moved almost of their own accord to rectify the situation, but he caught her hands in his and looped them around his neck once more.

"Patience, my lady," he said, reaching for

the wash cloth.

She closed her eyes as he stroked the cloth over her shoulders, down her throat, tracing her collarbone before caressing the tops of her breasts. Then the cloth was gone, replaced by his lips, kissing a trail of fire across her skin. Penelope threw her head back and moaned aloud.

He could just pick her up, push up her skirts and pin her against the wall. She would open to him like a flower to the sun, like a…

Like a prostitute in an alley, down by the docks.

The thought was his, not hers, but it was tinted with amusement. He was teasing her, deliberately imagining things that might make her change her mind. Almost as if he wished she would come to her senses and see him for what he was.

A brave, honourable knight who had come to save her when no one else would. Her knight, and now her husband.

She would meet his challenge, for she had read the thoughts of sailors and whores alike. And she intended to enjoy her first night with him far more than any prostitute who had to fake her pleasure for her customers' coin. "I believe 'tis cheaper to have stand-up sex in an alley than in a bed in a brothel. But if my husband insists, the alley behind the inn is empty at the moment…"

Godfrey's mouth dropped open with shock. He hadn't expected such salty language from his convent-raised lady. He recovered quickly. "When I make love to you for the first time, it shall be in a bed. For if you truly are determined to consummate this marriage, madness though it may be, I will give you no cause to regret your choice."

From levity to seriousness in a moment, yet even with her blood fair boiling with desire, she knew this was the wisest course. "I have no regrets," she said simply, undoing the lacings of her gown before he could stop her. Her clothes wilted to the floor, along with any whispering doubts she might have had. She stood naked before him, arms spread. "Behold, your willing bride."

He looked her up and down for a long moment, his thoughts revealing nothing but the curves of her body, pale skin that had never seen the sun now revealed in the lantern light for him alone.

"Just an ordinary woman. Not worth waging a war over." She managed a small smile, hoping her equally small jest might provoke some reaction from him.

He reached for the jug of wine, then poured himself a cup. He lifted it to his lips as he regarded her again. Godfrey drank deeply, his thoughts darting about her body like a swarm of bees. The silkiness of her skin, the pink pearls of her nipples, the tight curls at the juncture of her thighs, the weight of her breasts in his hands, the softness of her behind as he pulled her to him, the flush of her cheeks as her eyes kindled with desire, piercing his very soul with longing.

His soul, or hers? She wasn't sure any more where his thoughts ended and hers began.

"Restraint be damned. I cannot resist you any longer," he growled. He seized her and kissed her. She expected him to be rough, but his every movement was firm and deliberate. He would never hurt her.

She pressed against him, gasping as her tender nipples rasped against his tunic, a new one he'd brought from home. Better than being dressed like a friar, a man vowed to celibacy. That would never do.

It was her turn to lift his hem, to tug the tunic over his head and throw it onto the floor. Then her turn to gasp again as she traced the muscles he'd hidden beneath the shapeless garment. Why, he was built like the ancient statues, all hard ridges, but warm like no statue she'd ever seen. She hadn't believed it was possible to want him more, and yet…

He scooped her up effortlessly and tossed her onto the bed, where she found she could regard him properly, so she just lay back on her elbows and looked.

A wry smile twisted his lips, as he spread his arms wide, just as she had. "Behold, your knight without his armour."

Fine muscles indeed, with a trail of hair that led into his hose and further…hardness. Her cheeks heated again, searing her mouth to desert dryness. She wanted to tell him to take off his hose, to come to bed, to kiss her, to claim her, to do all the things he'd dreamed about and more, but her voice seemed to have died. "Please," she whispered, the only word she could say.

The hose vanished as if by magic, and he lay his body beside hers on the bed. He slid a finger under her chin, lifting her eyes to meet his, and all individual thoughts were lost. She was his, and he was hers, two waves crashing together in an ocean of desire that consumed them both. Utterly. Completely.

When the swirling, tempestuous waves within her reached their peak, she found her voice again, screaming Godfrey's name until she had no breath left. But he was there, kissing the breath back into her body, coaxing her to new, undreamed-of heights until he, too, shouted her name to the heavens, and it seemed that two souls were truly one.

Thirty-Eight

The sun was well and truly risen by the time Godfrey and Penelope managed to get the enchanted horse into the sky again. No matter how much he told himself they should hurry, he could not seem to bring himself to care. She was his willing wife, madness though it seemed, and no one could take away the pleasure they'd shared last night. Truly, he did not deserve her.

"What is THAT? It looks like…a wave coming in and swallowing the road, or…I don't know. And there's another one over there, too…"

Godfrey followed her pointing finger. "That's an army on the move. Two armies on the move. Both headed for Rialto." Dread curdled in his stomach. "But Rialto has warships and defences, right?" He peered across the water. "I can see the ships now!"

Penelope leaned forward, squinting. "Rialto has no warships at the moment, not since Duke Vitale died. Father hasn't commissioned a new war fleet yet. Those are Northmen vessels, built for rougher and deeper seas than ours. Which would mean…three armies headed for Rialto."

Her calm tone was maddening. Perhaps she didn't know what an army could do to a city. What the infidels had done to the Holy City. What the crusaders had done to…everywhere they went.

"We have to do something. Warn them. Or we won't be safe here." You won't be safe here.

Penelope shook her head. "Rialto is not like other cities. No army has ever taken it, and they will not do so now. We will fly to my father's palace, and tell him what is coming. And then…we wait. For them to send their envoys. Then the negotiations will begin."

"But they have armies…"

"Armies cannot walk on water, and those deep water ships cannot negotiate the shoals and shallows of the Rialto lagoon. There are not enough gondolas in the lagoon to transport one army, let alone three, and even then, they might not be willing to pay the boatmen's price." She patted Godfrey's arm. "I may not know much about swords or horses or battle, but I was born in Rialto, raised listening to merchants making bargains every minute of every day. When the envoys come, and they will, I will work out what they want, and are willing to sacrifice for it. I will tell you, and you will advise my father and his council accordingly. When there are three armies camped around Rialto, the safest place to be is Rialto itself. You shall see."

Either she was incredibly naïve, or she knew more about politics than Godfrey could even imagine. Neither was a particularly comforting thought, but, because he had no better plan, he headed for the Ducal Palace. For whatever the armies meant to do, he had a quest to fulfil.

265

Thirty-Nine

By the time they reached the Ducal Palace, Father was already busy with his council, and the reception hall was full of important people, also waiting their turn to see him.

Penelope settled in for a long wait, made more pleasant when the servants recognised her and brought refreshments.

"How long will this take?" Godfrey asked, peering at the other groups, unaware that he'd said the same thing as three other men at almost the exact same time.

Penelope shrugged. "As long as it takes. It

looks like the armies sent envoys ahead of them, and most of them are already here. The Northmen…they are upset because they heard Emperor Frederick's son was to marry me instead of their king's sister, as there is a longstanding betrothal. All Emperor Frederick has to do is agree to celebrate the marriage immediately, and they will be satisfied.

"Now, Frederick's people are less easy to please. Your father received Count Vesone's letter, and sent his answer to Prince Magnus, who considers his refusal a great insult to himself and his father. He has persuaded his brothers and their army to support him, but all he really wants is to marry some woman other than the Northmen's king's sister. I think the betrothal is with his older brother, anyway, but I can't be sure.

"Oh, and there's the matter of Frederick's claim to the title of Emperor. It appears the present Pope has not approved it, and Frederick is willing to negotiate with him to make things official. But in order to do that, he'll need the support of the Northmen, and Rialto. Perhaps even Emperor Manuel, as well.

So even if they've ostensibly come here at Magnus's insistence, they have more important things to discuss.

"The army from Byzas…now they're interesting. The Emperor still holds our people in his prison, but he's willing to negotiate for their release if we hand him…hmm, I believe he wants the magician. And possibly his flying horse. He's come here in search of him because Gabrieli admitted to being from Rialto, and he was headed this way when he left Byzas.

"Ah, but Emperor Manuel has a problem. If he releases our people, they will demand compensation for their stolen goods and businesses, and that will beggar the royal treasury, so he will be willing to do anything for gold to fill those empty coffers, up to and including marrying his young sons to rich women. The Northmen bride comes with a crown, but little dowry, which is why he wanted me. When he finds out I am already married, he will look elsewhere — likely to Emperor Frederick, who might have an eligible daughter or two. Manuel's daughter might do for Magnus — she's old enough for marriage, and has a peculiar hobby involving torture implements in her father's dungeons, so the two of them should get along nicely.

"So…with a few marriage alliances, and a fair bit of gold changing hands, we can probably send most of them away from here, not entirely unhappy."

Godfrey shook his head. He would never understand politics like she did. Never. "And what does Rialto want?"

She smiled. "Oh, the same as always. More autonomy, fewer tariffs and taxes. More opportunities to make money. My father and his council are all from good merchant families — they will act to further Rialto's trade interests. Merely hosting these negotiations will increase Rialto's power immeasurably, for it is in all their interests to see Rialto endure, to prolong the peace."

"And what about the Pope? What will he want?"

Penelope laughed. "A man of God, head of the church…I am sure he wants many holy things, as is proper. But most of all, he will want a new crusade, particularly after the failure of this last one, and he knows Rialto is the best port to launch one from. If Rialto calls, he will come, and at least listen to what these kings and emperors have to say. So that when he or his successor calls for another crusade, Rialto will rebuild its war fleet, and answer his call."

"Lady Penelope, Duke Sebastiano will see you now."

This earned them the animosity of most of the other men in the room, but this didn't seem to bother Penelope. She followed her father's man to his office, where she abandoned all decorum and ran to embrace her father.

The Duke did not want to let her go, holding her at arm's length as he studied her face, her clothes, and even her boots.

"Are you well?" he asked cautiously.

Penelope laughed. "Well enough to try to sell a man the finest Rialto lace, so fine only men who are truly noble may see it. My ill luck that Count Vesone was an honest man, who thought me mad when he could not see the cloth."

The Duke managed a weak smile. "And the rogue who kidnapped you?"

"Gabrieli is dead. Slain by Magnus, one of Emperor Frederick's sons. I believe Emperor Manuel offered his daughter in marriage to the man who could bring him Gabrieli's head, so you might want to suggest the alliance yourself."

Sebastiano nodded thoughtfully. "I suspect you have quite a tale to tell. I fear I have little time to spare today, but if your tale might help to explain why three armies are circling our fair city, perhaps I must make the time."

The Duke called for refreshments, before Penelope and Godfrey told their tale.

Finally, Godfrey reached the part where they'd arrived at his father's house, and reached over to pour another cup of wine, but the jug was empty.

"I fear there is little more to tell, Father, for I know you are busy. I have never seen your reception hall so full," Penelope said.

Sebastiano nodded, then turned to Godfrey. "Thank you. I cannot express how grateful I am that you brought her back. If there is ever anything I can do for you..."

Godfrey swallowed. It was now or never. "There is only one thing I would ask of you. A small thing, really. I – "

"We," Penelope interrupted, squeezing Godfrey's hand.

"We would like to ask you to bless our marriage."

Father suddenly grew very still. Then he shook himself and said, "Sir Godfrey, would you be so kind as to take the wine jug and find a servant who will refill it? I can't imagine where they have all gone to."

Godfrey glanced at her and registered her slight nod before taking the wine jug. "Of course, Monsignor."

He slipped out of the room.

Father considered several suitable ways to start the conversation, but Penelope had waited long enough.

She wet her lips. "The Byzas princes are children, their treasury is empty, and it is only a matter of time before a palace coup occurs. Frederick's elder sons might be nice enough, but they have a feudal government that we have no desire to see here. To marry one of them would put Rialto at risk. Gabrieli, Marco, and all the young merchants or merchants' sons here…they would want my dowry, and even I know it was lost somewhere in the northern seas. My brothers would not allow you to beggar the family business to make another family rich. Was there ever anyone you considered good enough to marry me?"

Father sighed. "You're right. No, I never met a man I considered good enough for you. The one thing you asked me for, a husband who will make you happy, that I cannot give you."

"Sir Godfrey makes me happy. He searched everywhere until he found me, and stole me from under the nose of Prince Magnus himself, who planned to force me into marriage."

"But…a horse trader?"

Penelope smiled. "We visited his family home. His father is a feudal baron, it's true, but Godfrey has older brothers who will inherit the title, while he is merely a knight. And the horses – such horses! The finest ever bred. Emperor Frederick knows the value of them already, and Emperor Manuel can be made to know it, in time. There is some value in being the merchant who represents both the buyers' and the breeders' interests, particularly when many of them are kings."

"You should have been born a boy. I swear, you are more astute than your brothers, when it comes to some things."

"But then I wouldn't be able to be your favourite daughter. Or Sir Godfrey's wife."

Father's forehead crinkled. "Do you truly wish to marry the man? Will he make you happy?"

Penelope rose. "Godfrey and I are already married, and he does make me happy." And if you give us your blessing, we will stay until the peace treaties are signed, but if you do not, we shall leave, she thought as she fixed her gaze on her father.

He sighed. "I will tell the servants to prepare a guest apartment for you both here in the palace. I have plans for the campo, and I would love to ask you what you think."

Penelope beamed. "Thank you, Father."

Forty

The summer sun shone on Penelope's bare feet as she dangled them over the canal. The enchanted horse lurked beneath the surface, ready to be buried and forgotten when the canal was filled in on the morrow.

She reached for another peach. The trees had been moved to another island, and where they had once grown was now covered in cobblestones, set in such a way that they looked like fish scales. Soon, the whole campo, including the canal beneath her feet, would be paved over to become Saint Mark's Square, where two emperors, a Northman king, the Pope, and her father would sign the peace treaties that divided the world between them. Three princes and three princesses would be married, and the hostilities would be over.

They would all stay to witness the annual ceremony where the Duke walked out to the edge of the sandbank protecting the city and said the city's marriage vows to the sea. This year, the Pope had not only agreed to officiate, but he'd given the Duke a gold ring to throw into the water to signify how he blessed the union.

It seemed almost an anticlimax to have weddings instead of a big battle, but that's how things were done in the Republic of Rialto.

"What do you want to do next?" Godfrey asked Penelope.

She threw her peach stone into the canal. "Hope there is something cool to drink in the kitchen. It used to be lovely here under the trees, but now the sun beats down on you unmercifully."

He chuckled. "I mean after the treaties are signed. Would you like to live here, or come home with me, where we can ride every day, or did you have some other adventure in mind?"

Penelope considered. "I would like to spend the rest of the summer somewhere cooler. And there's my dowry…My brothers used it to finance a shipping expedition to the northern seas, but the ship and cargo were taken by pirates, after reaching Beacon Isle. Once the treaty is signed, we could find a ship headed to northern waters, and see if we can find my dowry…along with the rest of the pirate treasure."

Godfrey laughed, then realised she hadn't joined him. "You mean you are serious?"

Penelope shrugged. "It's a sizeable sum. Well worth tracking down, so that any children we have might have the money to join my family business in Rialto, if that is their wish, or buy more breeding stock for your horse herds." She smiled. "More importantly, it is another adventure, where we will not have to worry about saving one another. Just…enjoy things as they happen. Will you take me on an adventure, Sir Godfrey? Just a knight and his lady, no one else?"

He could not refuse her anything, and she knew it. "If you want an adventure, my lovely lady wife, then you shall have one. I hear the pirates around Beacon Isle are quite lovely this time of year."

About the Author

Demelza Carlton has always loved the ocean, but on her first snorkelling trip she found she was afraid of fish.

She has since swum with sea lions, sharks and sea cucumbers and stood on spray drenched cliffs over a seething sea as a seven-metre cyclonic swell surged in, shattering a shipwreck below.

Demelza now lives in Perth, Western Australia, the shark attack capital of the world.

The *Ocean's Gift* series was her first foray into fiction, followed by her suspense thriller *Nightmares* trilogy. She swears the *Mel Goes to Hell* series ambushed her on a crowded train and wouldn't leave her alone.

Want to know more? You can follow Demelza on Facebook, Twitter, YouTube or her website, Demelza Carlton's Place at:

www.demelzacarlton.com

Books by Demelza Carlton

Siren of Secrets series
Ocean's Secret (#1)
Ocean's Gift (#2)
Ocean's Infiltrator (#3

Siren of War series
Ocean's Justice (#1)
Ocean's Widow (#2)
Ocean's Bride (#3)
Ocean's Rise (#4)
Ocean's War (#5)
How To Catch Crabs

Nightmares Trilogy
Nightmares of Caitlin Lockyer (#1)
Necessary Evil of Nathan Miller (#2)
Afterlife of Alana Miller (#3)

Mel Goes to Hell series
The Devil's Work (#1)
See You in Hell (#2)
Mel Goes to Hell (#3)
To Hell and Back (#4)
The Holiday From Hell (#5)
All Hell Breaks Loose (#6)
The Devil Goes to Heaven (#7)

Romance Island Resort series

Maid for the Rock Star (#1)
The Rock Star's Email Order Bride (#2)
The Rock Star's Virginity (#3)
The Rock Star and the Billionaire (#4)
The Rock Star Wants A Wife (#5)
The Rock Star's Wedding (#6)
Maid for the South Pole (#7)

Romance a Medieval Fairytale series

Enchant: Beauty and the Beast Retold
Dance: Cinderella Retold
Fly: Goose Girl Retold
Revel: Twelve Dancing Princesses Retold
Silence: Little Mermaid Retold
Awaken: Sleeping Beauty Retold
Embellish: Brave Little Tailor Retold
Appease: Princess and the Pea Retold
Blow: Three Little Pigs Retold
Return: Hansel and Gretel Retold
Wish: Aladdin Retold
Melt: Snow Queen Retold
Spin: Rumpelstiltskin Retold
Kiss: Frog Prince Retold
Reflect: Snow White Retold
Roar: Goldilocks Retold
Cobble: Elves and the Shoemaker Retold
Float: Enchanted Horse Retold
Steal: Forty Thieves Retold
Call: Pied Piper Retold